DEKOK AND THE
BROTHERS OF THE EASY DEATH

"DeKok" Books by A.C. Baantjer:

Published in the United States:
Murder in Amsterdam
DeKok and the Sunday Strangler
DeKok and the Corpse on Christmas Eve
DeKok and the Somber Nude
DeKok and the Dead Harlequin
DeKok and the Sorrowing Tomcat
DeKok and the Disillusioned Corpse
DeKok and the Careful Killer
DeKok and the Romantic Murder
DeKok and the Dying Stroller
DeKok and the Corpse at the Church Wall
DeKok and the Dancing Death
DeKok and the Naked Lady
DeKok and the Brothers of the Easy Death
DeKok and Murder on the Menu

Available soon from InterContinental Publishing:
DeKok and the Deadly Accord
DeKok and Murder in Seance
DeKok and Murder in Ecstasy
DeKok and the Begging Death
DeKok and the Geese of Death
DeKok and Murder by Melody
DeKok and Death of a Clown
DeKok and Variations on Murder
DeKok and Murder by Installments
DeKok and Murder on Blood Mountain
DeKok and the Dead Lovers
DeKok and the Mask of Death
DeKok and the Corpse by Return
DeKok and Murder in Bronze
DeKok and the Deadly Warning
DeKok and Murder First Class
DeKok and the Vendetta
DeKok and Murder Depicted
DeKok and Dance Macabre
DeKok and the Disfiguring Death
DeKok and the Devil's Conspiracy
DeKok and the Duel at Night
and more . . .

DeKok and the Brothers of the Easy Death

by
BAANTJER

translated from the Dutch by H.G. Smittenaar

INTERCONTINENTAL PUBLISHING

ISBN 1 881164 13 6

Printing History:
> 1st Dutch printing: 1979
> 2nd Dutch printing: 1979
> 3rd Dutch printing: 1980
> 4th Dutch printing: 1984
> 5th Dutch printing: 1985
> 6th Dutch printing: 1987
> 7th Dutch printing: 1989
> 8th Dutch printing: 1990
> 9th Dutch printing: 1991
> 10th Dutch printing: 1991
> 11th Dutch printing: 1992
> 12th Dutch printing: 1992
> 13th Dutch printing: 1993
> 14th Dutch printing: 1994
> 15th Dutch printing: 1995
>
> 1st American edition: 1995

Typography: Monica S. Rozier
Cover Photo: Peter Coene

DeKok
and the
Brothers of the Easy Death

1

Detective-Inspector DeKok of the Amsterdam Municipal Police (Homicide) paced up and down the large, busy detective room of the old, renowned police station at 48 Warmoes Street. It was one of his habits. He liked to walk. He did it often. By preference he walked through the narrow streets and along the old canals of his beloved Amsterdam and when he was inside, he liked to pace. The cadence of his steps helped to organize his thoughts. His broad, craggy face with the friendly expression of a good-natured boxer looked serious. Suddenly he stopped in front of Vledder's desk. Vledder looked up at his old partner.

"What's the matter with you?" asked the young man. "You seem unusually restless, somber even."

DeKok looked down at the eager young face and shook his head as if trying to clear it. Then he resumed his pacing.

Vledder followed him with his eyes, a bemused smile on his face. He and DeKok had worked together for some time and usually with success. DeKok was probably the best-known cop in all of Holland. Some of his cases had been spectacular. But with all that notoriety, DeKok had remained himself. An anachronism who longed for a time at least one hundred years ago. He disliked most modern conveniences and he seemed to stumble his way through investigations. So far, however, thought Vledder, DeKok had always caught the perpetrators and his final reports always resulted in a conviction.

Vledder thought back to the first time he had worked with the gray sleuth. It had been a case of murdered prostitutes. The police, including Vledder, with all their technical know-how and sophisticated equipment had been unable to solve the case. In desperation, Vledder had suggested re-calling DeKok from his vacation. The old man had arrived and in a matter of days, without any apparent effort, had solved the case. He had used the same methods he had used for more than twenty-five years, augmented by experience and a thorough knowledge of the city he loved so much. It had been a revelation to Vledder and he had managed to remain permanently assigned to DeKok. First as an assistant and than as partner. But through it all, in Vledder's eyes, DeKok had always remained his mentor.

The station, situated at the edge of Amsterdam's Red Light District, was considered the busiest police station in Europe. Vledder had heard that there was a station near the harbor in Marseille that was supposed to be busier, but it had never, to his knowledge, been referred to as the French "Hill Street". A sobriquet that had been applied many times to Warmoes Street.

The Red Light District, or the Quarter as it is known by the locals, is located in the oldest part of Amsterdam and it is generally accepted that Warmoes Street is the oldest street in the town. And beside everything else, thought Vledder, the police station is probably the oldest, draftiest and most decrepit building on Warmoes Street.

DeKok stopped again in front of his desk and raked his fingers through his hair.

"I can't accept it," he growled. "I just can't. I have the feeling that someone is playing with us . . . making a macabre joke."

"Some joke." Vledder smiled bitterly. "The humor escapes me. I don't think that two corpses are a joke. Do you really think they have been murdered?"

DeKok shrugged his mighty shoulders.

"That's exactly my problem. It was all so peaceful, so without violence. You might even call it an 'idyllic' suicide."

"Double suicide?"

"That's not so strange," gestured DeKok. "There are plenty of examples. I have dealt with a few myself."

"Hand in hand?"

DeKok nodded.

"Certainly. Only the means differed. They either took the same poison . . . or gassed themselves. There have been some satanic shooting arrangements that would insure that both would die at the same time."

Vledder shook his head.

"Idiots . . . why go to all that trouble?"

"Keep in mind," said DeKok slowly, "that suspicion is a real factor with a double suicide."

"Suspicion?"

"Sure . . . suspicion of the partner, suspicion whether or not the other will go through with it . . . planning to live on by himself, or herself. It's not exactly an easy decision . . . to plan a double suicide. People want to be sure the other goes through with it."

"Even in a case of drowning?"

DeKok shook his head.

"That's exactly my problem. I've never run across that before." His tone was irritated. "There are no examples, as far as I know. It's just so hard to imagine." He paused and scratched the tip of his nose. "Let's assume for the moment," he continued, "that the Shoebeek couple did indeed plan to commit a double suicide, driven by some vague conception of 'until death do us part.' Together they walk down to Emperors Canal, take each other by the arm, entwine their fingers and jump." He sighed. "Apart from the fact that practically every Dutch citizen knows how to swim and regardless of the strength of their death wish, there had to be an immediate reflex, an involuntary action by the body, bent on preserving itself, as soon as they hit the cold water." He looked at the young Inspector. "You see, they would let go of each other."

Vledder's eyes widened in understanding.

"And they were found arm in arm."

DeKok nodded sadly.

"Arm in arm and with tightly entwined fingers."

"Like young lovers."

"Exactly."

Both remained silent for a while. A ballast hummed in one of the light fixtures on the ceiling and the raucous sounds from the Quarter penetrated through the windows behind DeKok's desk. Vledder finally broke the silence between them.

"Is there going to be an autopsy?"

DeKok grabbed a chair and placed it near the desk of the younger man. He sat down.

"I urged it," he said, "and the Commissaris*, for once, agreed with me. He called, but the Judge-Advocate saw no reason. There were also objections from the family. Something about religious concerns . . . complications involving the Final Judgement. As a matter of fact, they approached the Judge-Advocate before the Commissaris had even reached him and apparently he had already promised. In any case, he rejected my

---

* Commissaris: a rank equivalent to Captain. There are only two ranks higher: Chief-Commissaris and Chief Constable. Each jurisdiction has only a single Chief Constable, the highest possible police rank. There is one Chief Constable for all of Amsterdam. Other ranks in the Municipal Police are: Constable, Constable First Class, Sergeant, Adjutant, Inspector, Chief-Inspector and Commissaris. Adjutants and below are equivalent to non-commissioned ranks. Inspector is a rank equivalent to 2nd Lieutenant.

suggestion for a judicial autopsy and asked if there were indications that foul play was involved. And there are no such indications, at least not at this time. There were no signs of any violence on the bodies of Mr. and Mrs. Shoebeek. Dr. Koning did a thorough job, but he couldn't even discover a puncture mark. They were, as they say, completely whole."

"So," snorted Vledder, "suicide by drowning?"

"Exactly," nodded DeKok. "Suicide by drowning. There was no other conclusion to be drawn."

"And what about you?"

"What do you mean?"

"What sort of conclusion did you come to?"

DeKok rubbed the bridge of his nose with a little finger. Then he stared at it for a while. Finally he lowered his hand and searched his pockets. Vledder waited patiently. DeKok was looking for candy. The old man had a decided sweet tooth and always seemed to have various pieces of candy stashed away in his pockets. DeKok unearthed a toffee and looked at it with satisfaction. Slowly he unwrapped the sticky wrapper and popped the sweet in his mouth. The wrapper was rolled into a tiny ball and dropped in a convenient trash can. Only then did he answer Vledder.

"I just don't know," he said thoughtfully, sucking on the toffee. "I find it very hard to believe in a double suicide. There are no signs, no indications, no preparations. The couple had just returned from a winter vacation in Cortina d'Ampezzo. I saw the pictures . . . relaxed, happy people, a glass of wine in their hands, a smile on their faces. There is no last will and testament and there are no indications that a suicide was ever contemplated before. I talked to the couple's only son. Although he was, in his words, forced to believe in suicide, he found the very notion absurd. They were simply two dear, normal people in their fifties who got along just fine . . ."

11

"Rich?" interrupted Vledder.

"No," denied DeKok. "He was employed by a bank. A comfortable income, but nothing extravagant. Head of some sort of department at the bank."

"Debts?"

"None . . . nothing significant. I asked the bank to check everything carefully. They lived well within their means and there was no hint of fraud. Shoebeek was a valued employee."

"An incurable disease?"

DeKok grinned crookedly. With a tired gesture he raked his fingers through his hair.

"You are asking all the right questions," he commented. "But no, I checked with their physician. Both were in perfect health."

Vledder shook his head in exasperation.

"No motives for suicide," he repeated to himself. Suddenly he looked at his old partner. "What about murder?"

DeKok rose slowly from his chair.

"But who would possibly want to kill two dear people in their fifties who got along so well together and . . ." He did not complete the sentence.

His eyes went to the door of the detective room. A young woman appeared in the doorway and paused there for effect, one hand on her hip, the pelvis pushed slightly forward. With a patronizing movement she turned to the detective nearest the door and asked him a question. The man nodded with his head in DeKok's direction and she pirouetted gracefully around her axis. With calm, deliberate steps and sensuous movements she walked across the room. Some of the men looked at her with desire and most of the female detectives looked at her with a certain amount of envy. She moved like a model on a runway. Every step deliberate, every gesture provocative.

DeKok held his breath. She was beautiful, he found, extremely beautiful, almost classical with an abundance of exciting curves and shapes. She carried her head high and her gold-blonde hair cascaded down to the collar of a short, red jacket.

DeKok wondered if he knew her, if he had met her before. Hastily he searched his memory but could not place her, his retentive memory held no reference to her. With a fleeting, melancholy thought he reflected that he had met so many beautiful, blonde women in his long career. Somehow they all looked alike . . . very blonde, very beautiful and very Dutch. Not surprising, he thought, since this is Holland. But although they all seemed to look alike, they never failed to arouse the same initial mesmerizing effect on him. He hoped that it would remain that way for a long time. DeKok approved of women.

With a hesitating, almost shy, gesture she stretched out a hand toward him.

"My name is Monique . . . Monique Vankerk."

Her voice was warm and melodious and did not lose its effect on the gray sleuth. He swallowed. Carefully he pressed the outstretched hand.

"DeKok," he said, "with . . . eh, with kay-oh-kay." He pointed at Vledder. "My colleague, Dick Vledder."

She nodded curtly in the direction of the young Inspector, dismissing him at the same time as she acknowledged him.

"At first I was afraid to come," she confessed softly, looking at DeKok. "I waited, hesitated for some time. I mean, you see, Warmoes Street has a . . . a certain reputation. It's not a very nice part of town, is it?"

DeKok gave her a winning smile. His enchantment had vanished and the professionalism of the experienced detective took over.

"I assure you," he said soothingly, "the reputation of Warmoes Street . . . and the Quarter, is very much exaggerated. There's a lot of innuendo and gossip. Some of the more disreputable papers . . ." He did not finish the sentence but held a chair for her with an old-fashioned, courteous gesture. "Please sit down," he invited.

She hesitated again, looked at Vledder.

"I . . . eh, I would prefer to speak with you in private."

DeKok smiled reassuringly.

"Be at ease," he said. "Vledder and I have no secrets from each other and we're both bound by our oath."

She sat down carefully, crossed her long, slender legs and pulled her skirt down over her knees.

"I . . . eh," she hesitated, "I want to request . . . my husband is missing and I want him found."

DeKok gave her a long, searching look.

"Any reason to worry?"

Monique Vankerk flicked her tongue along the full, red lips.

"Richard left exactly one week ago. The first of February. Since then I haven't heard a thing from him, seen hide nor hair."

"Did he often stay away for a few days?"

She shook her head.

"It never happened before. Ever since we've been married, we've never spent a night apart."

DeKok bit his lip, suppressed a naughty remark.

"Did you check with the family?"

Monique made a vague gesture.

"There's no sense in that, no use at all. Richard hasn't had any contact with his family for years. Because they refused to accept me as his wife, Richard broke all ties with them."

"But you married anyway?"

She nodded with emphasis.

14

"Richard and I married very formally in the old town hall at Rijp. Just to be sure, I brought a copy of our marriage certificate."

DeKok waved that away.

"Children?"

She shook her head. A sad expression came over her face.

"Richard never wanted any. He felt he was too old."

DeKok's eyebrows rippled briefly in that uncanny manner of his. Monique blinked her eyes, unable to believe what she had seen. Vledder watched carefully. He took a silent delight in watching the reaction of people who were confronted with the amazing gymnastics DeKok's eyebrows could display.

"Too old?" repeated DeKok, disbelief in his voice.

She opened her purse and took a photograph from it. She handed it to DeKok. It was the picture of a well-preserved man in his fifties with a small moustache and charming gray at the temples.

"Richard was married before," she explained. "I'm his second wife. The first must have been a horrible woman."

"Died?"

"No. Divorced, years ago. But every once in a while she still bothers him."

DeKok cocked his head at her.

"Could his disappearance have anything to do with his first wife?"

"How?"

"Alimony." DeKok gestured. "Financial complications."

Monique shrugged her shapely shoulders.

"It's all so confusing, so strange . . . so, so uncertain. I just don't know what to think. I'm afraid."

DeKok ignored the remark. He often had a way of ignoring things in a way that could bring people to tears, depending on

15

one's point of view. According to Vledder, it was one of his least likeable habits. He watched as DeKok stared at the woman.

"When your husband left the house, last week," continued DeKok after a long silence, "where was he planning to go?"

She vaguely indicated a direction.

"To the bank close by, around the corner. On the canal. He had to get some money."

"And did he go to the bank?"

She closed her eyes momentarily and sighed deeply.

"Yes, he was in the bank."

"And he made a withdrawal, took out cash?"

"Yes, I suppose so."

"What do you mean," pounced DeKok, "you suppose so?"

She moved uneasily in her chair.

"When I went to ask, they . . . the people at the bank . . . they were sort of secretive. They didn't want to tell me how much he had withdrawn. But I *did* get the impression it wasn't exactly a small sum."

"Did he have to make any large cash payments?"

Her well-manicured nails drummed on the top of the desk.

"I don't know." She sounded irked. "Richard never told me anything about his business. He kept me out of that part of his life. Maybe . . . maybe I just wasn't interested enough. But I do know that he always used the bank to make payments. He never needed cash for that."

"Did your husband gamble?"

"You mean . . . roulette, or cards?"

"Exactly."

Monique Vankerk shook her head decisively.

"No, that wasn't his style. Maybe he gambled a bit in the stock market, but always conservatively. Playing the market, he called it. That's what it was, I think, play."

Young Vledder leaned forward.

"Perhaps your husband is having an affair . . . is there another woman?"

She reacted as if bitten by a snake. She jumped up. Her face was red and her eyes flashed.

"Richard doesn't chase after women. He's a normal, considerate husband."

DeKok intervened, soothing her with his tone, as well as with the words.

"We're only trying to help," he said softly. "We're looking for a motive that might explain the sudden disappearance of your husband. Another woman *could* be such a motive."

She looked at him, angrily.

"There's no other woman." It sounded sharp and convincing.

DeKok rubbed the bridge of his nose with a little finger. She followed the movement of his hand and slowly re-seated herself.

"You were happily married?" asked DeKok.

Something seemed to snap within her. She found a minuscule handkerchief and held it to her eyes. He saw her shoulders shake. DeKok allowed her to regain her composure. After a while he gently placed a hand under her chin, forcing her to look in his eyes.

"You're worried about an accident?" he asked in a friendly tone of voice.

She shook her head sadly, still sobbing.

"I'm thinking of murder."

2

Young Inspector Vledder made a theatrical gesture with his arms.

"I'm thinking of murder." He mockingly imitated Monique's voice. Then he grinned and changed his tone. "But why would she think about murder? She hasn't said anything in that connection that made sense. No facts." He pointed at the picture on his desk. "And did you take a good look at the face of that man? The eyes, the lips, the small moustache . . . the typical hedonist, a bon-vivant. If you ask me, he took his savings out of the bank and took off with another woman."

DeKok cocked his head at his young colleague.

"To tell you the truth," he observed mildly, "I thought Monique Vankerk was extremely attractive."

"I see. You mean when you have steak at home, you don't need to find sandwiches in the street."

"Inelegant, but essentially correct."

"According to the theories, all beautiful blonde women live lives of unending bliss," grinned Vledder. "But you know as well as I do, that it's just not so. Even husbands of beautiful women will step outside the bonds of matrimony from time to time."

DeKok nodded agreement.

"And yet," he said, "I'm inclined to take Monique at face value. Don't underestimate a woman's intuition. She was positive that there was no other woman involved and she showed an inner conviction when she said her husband had been murdered."

Vledder was irritated and it showed in his voice.

"But what did she have in the way of facts? Nothing, absolutely nothing at all. She's been married for six years. Well, men get an itch every seven years or so. The seven-year itch. It's a well-known phenomenon. They even made a movie about it." He placed a hand flat on his chest. "And we should worry about that?"

"Murder is a crime."

Vledder was getting red.

"Who's talking about murder?" he demanded angrily.

The gray sleuth looked at him with unfeigned surprise.

"You heard her yourself," he answered. "Monique Vankerk."

Vledder made a gesture as if throwing something away.

The telephone rang and he changed the direction of his hand and picked up the receiver. After a few seconds he covered the mouthpiece and looked at DeKok.

"It's for you. It's the desk-sergeant, downstairs. He has a Brother Crispin and he wants to talk to you."

"The sergeant, or the Brother?"

"The Brother, of course."

"Tell them to send him up."

A few minutes later he entered: A slender young man with short, curly blond hair, dressed in a black suit of an expensive cut, a sparkling white shirt and a pearl-gray necktie. He had the open look of a man driven by certainty. Without asking directions, he crossed the busy detective room and aimed straight for DeKok with outstretched hand.

"Crispin," he said in a jubilant voice. "Brother Crispin of the Community of the Brothers and Sisters of the Holy Blessings."

The gray sleuth shook hands.

"DeKok," he said. He scratched the bridge of his nose with a little finger, then he added: "That's quite a mouthful. I don't think I can remember all that."

Brother Crispin nodded with a serious expression on his face.

"You're right. Indeed, you're right. The name *is* a bit long. That is why I usually just say The Community of the B&S of the HB. It's simpler. I also call us the Blessed Brothers and Sisters." He laughed and displayed two rows of healthy white teeth. "The name matters little . . . as long as we, as humans, will recognize and acknowledge God's Blessings. You see, that is our message, make yourself receptive, open yourself to the Blessings. That demands a strong and cheerful character and we want to strengthen that ability in people."

DeKok seemed impressed.

"A noble pursuit."

Vledder pricked up his ears. DeKok, as most good cops, genuinely liked people. But Vledder had detected a coldness in his voice that he had seldom heard before. Brother Crispin seemed oblivious. He looked toward the ceiling, half closing his eyes.

"There's a spiral that leads upward. The Spiral Road, as someone once said very eloquently."

"Jan de Hartog," interrupted DeKok, who admired that author.

"Exactly," continued the Brother blithely. "And through a positive outlook, with a happy heart, so to speak, one can discover the Blessings. And when the Blessings are discovered, it strengthens the gaiety of the spirit, the lightness of heart . . . which all result in a sharper observation of the Holy Blessings."

"Admirable."

Brother Crispin imparted a grateful look.

"Isn't it?"

DeKok looked long and hard at the Brother.

"Crispin," he asked after a long pause, "is that a Christian name, or a surname."

"Crispin is my baptismal name. My worldly name is Peter Jaarsma."

DeKok nodded his understanding.

"I don't presume that you came to Warmoes Street in order to convert me to your religion?"

Brother Crispin smiled ecstatically. His blond head bobbed up and down in a mixture of gratification and subservience.

"That would truly be one of God's Blessings," he said. Then the jubilant tone disappeared as he went on: "But actually I came to talk to you about our Brother and Sister Shoebeek . . . God rest their souls . . . who came to such a tragic end. I understand that you're in charge of the inevitable administrative complications?"

"Yes."

Brother Crispin looked ill at ease as he came closer to the edge of his chair.

"You see, their deaths were totally unexpected. We have just organized a meeting for our Brother and Sister."

"A memorial service?"

Brother Crispin shook his head sadly.

"We have not been able to agree on that, yet. The Community, so to speak, is of two minds. Frankly, we're not even sure if they are entitled to a memorial service."

"Why not?" asked DeKok, looking surprised.

Brother Crispin licked his lips.

"Life is a Blessing," he said unctuously. "We are only borrowing the life that God gives us. We cannot dispose of it at will."

"You're thinking about suicide?"

Brother Crispin seemed confused.

"But . . . eh, I understand that all the indications are that . . . eh, that there is no other explanation."

"I have not closed the case," said DeKok sharply. "The file is still open." He looked at the man. "What sort of meeting was it supposed to be?"

"A general meeting in our temple at Duivendrecht, in the suburbs."

"In honor of Brother and Sister Shoebeek?"

"No," denied Crispin, "not in their honor . . . but at their express request . . . a special meeting."

DeKok leaned back and opened a drawer of his desk. He found a bag of licorice. He opened the bag and peered expectantly at the contents. After some deliberation he selected a large piece of salted licorice and popped it in his mouth. Then he carefully closed the bag again and replaced it in his desk drawer. He closed the drawer. Only then did he again address the Brother.

"At their express request?" he asked. The chewing motion of his jaws did not hide the hint of astonishment. "And when did they make that express request?"

"About a week ago."

DeKok was now openly amazed.

"But at that time they were both on holiday in Cortina d'Ampezzo."

Brother Crispin nodded.

"The Shoebeeks wrote to me from Cortina and asked for a general meeting upon their return."

"Why did they write to you?"

"I'm their pastor, the leader of the congregation."

"And why the meeting?"

Brother Crispin shrugged his shoulders. There was a pained look on his face.

"They did not mention that . . . not exactly, anyway. They wrote that they had experienced a shocking incident and desired to discuss it with the complete membership of the Community."

"What sort of experience?"

Brother Crispin spread his arms.

"An experience of faith . . . a soul-shocking event. We're very interested in that sort of phenomenon."

"Is that what they wrote . . . an experience of faith, a soul-shocking event?"

"Those are usually the subjects of our general meetings." Brother Crispin started to sound exasperated.

DeKok chewed thoughtfully on his licorice while he raked his hands through his hair.

"Apart from you and the Shoebeeks, who else knew about the meeting?"

"We all knew, of course. The letter was read at the previous meeting."

DeKok swallowed the licorice and said nothing for a long time. He merely stared at his visitor with a long, penetrating look. Only cops could stare at people that way, without any regard for the feelings of the person under observation. Brother Crispin squirmed under the look when DeKok suddenly smiled broadly.

"You know, Brother Crispin," said DeKok in a friendly tone of voice, "I still don't know the reason for your visit."

Brother Crispin cleared his throat. With some difficulty he recollected himself.

"It is customary," he said evenly, "that those who call for a general meeting, also assume the costs associated therewith.

That is why I wanted to contact the relatives of our dear departed Brother and Sister Shoebeek. The survivors, you see. The Shoebeeks were very much dedicated to the movement and were extremely devout."

DeKok pressed his lips together and slowly shook his head.

"I'm very sorry. There's no Will, no Testament. There are no bequests, if that's what you mean . . ."

Brother Crispin had the grace to blush. Hastily he came to his feet and without another word he left the room.

DeKok watched him go, a pensive look in his eyes. Somehow he had the feeling that in the near future he would meet Brother Crispin again.

He remained seated for a long time, then he suddenly moved and went over to the coat rack. In passing he grabbed the photograph from Vledder's desk and he had already placed his old, decrepit felt hat on his head when Vledder asked:

"Where are you going?"

"Out," said DeKok, hoisting himself into his raincoat. "I'm going to see Little Lowee. I've a bad taste in my mouth."

* * *

Sometimes a bald man is called "curly" and a tall man is called "shorty", but it was immediately apparent why Lowee was called Little Lowee. Little Lowee was small. He also owned a bar in the District and he and DeKok had known each other for years. It was a strange relationship. Lowee, at one time or another, had possibly broken every one of God's and Man's commandments. Yet there was a certain cordiality between him and DeKok, a friendship based on mutual respect and understanding for the position of the other although DeKok had been known to exploit the relationship in a shameless manner from time to time.

But Lowee never blamed him for that. In Lowee's opinion everybody had his foibles and DeKok, being a cop, was entitled to more foibles than most. In his heart Lowee approved wholeheartedly of the Law.

"Men needs the Law," he would exclaim, "without the Law we would have a mess on our hands." And then, with his twisted sense of logic, he would add: "How can you enjoy doing wrong, if you don't know what's right?"

Such homilies were usually spouted in Lowee's version of Dutch. His language was the language of the quarter. The language is a mixture of Amsterdam slang, thieves' language and gutter language mixed with many bastardizations of Yiddish, French, English and Malay. The Malay influence was brought about by the close relationship between Amsterdam and the former Dutch East-Indies (now Indonesia). Even the Dutch have trouble with Amsterdam "underworld" linguistics. There is a story that the wise guys of Amsterdam sent a wreath to the funeral of a particular prosecutor with the inscription "Triefel Rag Monus" on the ribbon. The very upper-class mourners thought it to be from some fraternity or other. The actual language means (freely translated): Good Luck, Garbage.

Lowee's establishment, as he likes to refer to it himself, is situated at the corner of Barn Alley. A small, intimate locality with diffused, soft-pink lights. A favorite meeting place for the ladies of the night. Here they rest, take a break, exchange experiences, sip their sickening sweet beverages and talk about their mutual concerns . . . the business of the Quarter.

DeKok went to the end of the bar and hoisted himself on the stool that had come to be regarded as his regular seat. From this vantage point he could look over the entire room and his back was covered at all times against any eventualities, such as the sudden, spontaneous fisticuffs between two competing practitioners of the world's oldest profession. Sometimes a girl would break the code, work for less than the going rate, or would not insist on the use of a condom. This would cause disagreements and could lead to bitter fights.

Little Lowee hastily wiped his hands on a convenient rag and asked his usual question.

"Same recipe?"

Without waiting for an answer he dove under the bar and emerged with a venerable bottle of cognac. There was always a fine bottle of cognac underneath Lowee's bar, a bottle specifically reserved for DeKok. As Lowee lined up the large snifters he nodded condescendingly in Vledder's direction.

Vledder took no offense. By now he was familiar with Lowee's ways and he knew that he was merely tolerated because he was accompanied by DeKok. He grinned to himself. If he ever showed up alone, he would probably be ignored. Lowee firmly believed in the right to refuse service to any cop of whom he did not approve. As far as Vledder knew the only cop Lowee approved of was DeKok.

DeKok watched with satisfaction as Lowee poured the golden liquid into the paper-thin glasses. Carefully he lifted the glass and warmed it in his hand while he inhaled the aroma. There was an expression of pure delight on his face. To DeKok cognac was more than just a drink. It was a ceremony, almost a sacrament, worthy of serious reverence.

Lowee looked at him with eager expectation.

"How is it?" he asked after DeKok had taken his first sip.

"Mag-ni-fi-cent," answered DeKok with emphasis.

The small barkeeper laughed happily.

"I thought so meself. I gotta whole case of it." He winked. "Gotta good price too."

The gray sleuth lifted his glass once more.

"*Proost*," he said, "to all children of thirsty parents." His face fell. "As long as it doesn't interfere with business."

Little Lowee took a sip himself. Then he replaced the glass on the counter top.

"I's glad to see you," he said with conviction. "I done missed you for some days." He looked at DeKok with knowing eyes. "I bet you got your hands full with the couple they fished from Emperors Canal."

"That too."

"Busy?"

"Crime is a business that knows no recession." DeKok gestured widely. "I wonder," he added mockingly, "who's in charge of that concern. He must be a workaholic."

"Satan."

DeKok reacted surprised at the sound of the voice, he turned his gaze away from Lowee and discovered Sister Emilia of the Salvation Army. The old woman held a bundle of tracts against her ample bosom. DeKok knew her well, as he knew almost everybody who lived and worked around the Quarter. He gave her a friendly nod.

"Perhaps you're right, Sister."

Vledder entered the conversation.

"It isn't the work of one man . . . one devil. It's the work of many, many individuals. A lot of franchises."

Sister Emilia gave the young man a penetrating look.

"But they all have one thing in common, young man, they've all been kissed by Satan."

Vledder turned back toward the bar. He wasn't up to a discussion with the quick-witted Sister.

DeKok bought a tract and crumpled the paper into one of the pockets of his raincoat. Then his hand went to an inside pocket and emerged with the picture of the missing Richard Vankerk. He placed the photo on the bar and tapped one corner.

"You know this guy? Ever seen him around?"

Little Lowee took the photo in his hands and studied it carefully. After a few seconds he returned it to DeKok.

"You wants him for something?"

"Yes."

"Must be for stealing big time," grinned Lowee.

"Why would I want him for fraud?" asked DeKok.

A sweet grin transformed Lowee's friendly, mousey face into something almost winsome.

"He's loaded."

"Easy with his money?"

"You can say that again."

"What's his name?"

"Uncle Rickie."

"Uncle Rickie?" repeated DeKok.

"Sure," said Lowee with simple conviction. "He's a regular john with Blonde Tina. I seen him lotsa times."

"When did you see him last?"

Lowee stared at the ceiling as if looking for inspiration.

"Last week," he allowed after a while. "Musta been the first of the month. He was waiting for Tina, right here at the bar. When she show up, they have a coupla drinks together and then they split."

"Morning . . . Evening?"

"Afternoon . . . about three."

"And after that?"

Lowee spread his arms in a gesture of acquiescence.

"Never seen him again, her neither."

3

They had one more glass of cognac and then left the cozy little bar. They joined the crowds on Rear Fort Canal. As usual it was busy in the District. The Red Light District is an international attraction and lures even those who do not intend to partake of the services it offers. Many are just curiosity seekers. They were surrounded by the sounds of a hundred languages and the intriguing smells of exotic foods mingled with the harsher smells of stale beer and booze. DeKok reflected that only in Amsterdam would one see a sign stating unabashedly: "100% pure pornography". The crowds in front of that sex-shop were larger than elsewhere. With a certain amount of melancholy and pity he watched the heroin whores offer their wasted bodies to all and sundry while the "professional" whores waited patiently behind their windows for the next client. Then they would state their price, close the curtains and conduct their business.

DeKok was more familiar than most with the scenery around him. He often longed for the easy conviviality of the past that had now largely been replaced by the addition of the heroin-whores, those pitiful creatures that sold their bodies in exchange for the next fix. Although they were now assured of their next fix because of the Dutch attempt to decriminalize drugs and thereby removing the profit motive, for most of them it was too late. Their habits had been formed in more ways than one. The established prostitutes and brothel keepers lived on a footing of barely concealed violence with the addicts. At first they too, had pitied the often young girls who had found themselves enslaved by a debilitating habit. But over time the pity had changed to hatred. Clients were ill-served by the "amateurs" and were often abused or robbed. The business as a whole suffered because of it. Only in Amsterdam, mused DeKok.

His musings were interrupted by Vledder.

"What did I tell you," said the young man. "I'm right. Richard Vankerk just stepped out with another woman."

The gray sleuth did not answer directly.

"It seems that way," he evaded. "According to Lowee our Richard has been a steady customer of Blonde Tina . . . for quite some time. In that case, why would he suddenly leave? To possess Tina as a woman, he only had to pay, no more. And if we can believe Lowee, he had plenty of money." He paused. "Also, the disappearance of Blonde Tina does not necessarily have anything to do with the disappearance of Richard Vankerk. The two events may be totally unrelated."

"Is Tina an addict?" asked Vledder.

"No." DeKok shook his head. "Not as far as I know. But as you know, heroin is nasty stuff and lately there's much too much of it available. It can change you overnight."

"That quick?"

"That's right, it's just a matter of taking the first dose. You're hooked for life."

They crossed a bridge and pressed through the crowds into Stove Alley. The crowds were gathered in front of yet another sex-shop. This shop seemed to feature exclusively imitation penises. A veritable forest of dildos crowded the primitive show window. DeKok glanced at them in passing and questioned seriously if some of the examples on display could really be used to penetrate the human body in any other way than with fatal results.

They stopped in the middle of the alley and DeKok looked up. He tapped Vledder on the shoulder and said:

"Come on my boy, we're going visiting."

"Where?" wondered Vledder.

"We're going to visit Lame Greta," smiled DeKok.

"And who is Lame Greta?"

DeKok pushed open the door of the ground floor apartment that led to a second apartment upstairs.

"Blonde Tina's actual mother."

"Actual mother?"

"Yes," nodded DeKok. "She never knew a real mother."

* * *

Lame Greta removed an invisible speck of dust from the table top and smoothed out the old-fashioned tablecloth. Her small, wrinkled hands were continuously in motion. She looked at DeKok, a gleam in her eyes.

"Such honor," she chirped, "DeKok himself in my humble abode."

"It's been a long time," admitted DeKok, "since I came here regularly."

"The last time," said Lame Greta, "was when Black Jane was murdered. You needed me then." There was gentle censure in her voice.

DeKok placed a hand on her bony shoulders.

"Without you I would never have caught the killer." He smiled. "I'm still very grateful for your help."

Greta turned her head to look at him.

"Are you in trouble again?"

"I don't know," shrugged DeKok. "I'm just starting and there's little to go on. A man has disappeared. Without a trace. Maybe you've heard of him. He's about fifty. His name is Richard Vankerk."

"Uncle Rickie."

"You know him?"

"Ach," gestured Greta. "It all depends what you mean by 'know.' He's been here a few times. Tina brought him around."

"Why?"

"He's her customer."

"Did she *pees** here?"

Greta gave him a pitying look.

"Rickie was a gentleman, a real gentleman. He wasn't about to use a whore's room. He always rented a suite in an expensive hotel. Very chic . . . complete with room service." She shook her head. "No, he just came to visit here. Politeness, you see. Because of everything I had done for Tina in the past."

"Were they very close?"

"You mean, was it more than the usual relationship between a whore and her john?"

"Exactly."

A sad smile softened her face.

"I think that Tina was in love with him."

DeKok rubbed the bridge of his nose with a little finger.

"Richard Vankerk is married," he said.

"I know."

"I met her," said DeKok, admiration in his voice. "A beautiful woman, extremely beautiful."

Lame Greta looked angry.

---

* pees (verb, pronounced "pays"): an untranslatable term, meaning to use a place for the reception and entertainment of paying sex-clients. The same term is used to indicate the user, as well as the provider of the apartment, room, or hotel.

"A snake," she hissed. "A she-devil. Why do you think that Uncle Rickie took up with my Tina?" She snorted her contempt. "Because his wife won't let him, won't give him any. It's been like that for years. At night she locks herself in her bedroom and when he knocks on the door and begs to be admitted, she laughs at him."

DeKok made a denigrating gesture.

"That doesn't mean a thing," he protested, "every john has some sort of story to justify visiting the District. He'll slander his own wife, if necessary. It's an old story."

Lame Greta pressed her lips together as if refusing to say any more. Then she relented.

"DeKok, believe me," she said patiently. "I don't care how beautiful his wife is, she's no good, a bitch. You know what they say: Beauty is only skin deep, but ugly is rotten to the core. And that she is, rotten to the core. I've been in this business for more years than I care to remember and I know about johns. But Rickie is blameless. He was happily married, a nice wife and two grown children. Then she came into the picture. Oh, sure, in the beginning she was as willing as a squinting virgin with flat feet. He could do what he wanted. But once she had him hooked, it was all over with the love, *fini* . . . he could sleep on the rug at the foot of her bed, for all she cared."

DeKok smiled at her eloquence.

"How did they meet?"

"I don't know. I never asked, Rickie is rather vague about it."

"How does he come by his money?"

"If there's one thing you learn in this business," grimaced Greta, "it's never to ask about a john's money. Tina doesn't know either, and she doesn't want to know."

"Any idea?"

"Not a clue."

35

DeKok raked his fingers through his gray hair.

"They say that they haven't seen Tina for about a week."

"Who are they?" asked Greta sharply.

"In the neighborhood," answered DeKok vaguely.

Lame Greta sighed deeply.

"I was thinking about coming to see you," she confessed.

"Why?"

"I'm afraid, DeKok." A tic developed on her scrawny face. "I don't really want to present myself stronger than I am, but I'm afraid something has happened to her. You see, she just left. Without saying goodbye." A tear gleamed in her eyes. "That's not the way my Tina usually behaves. I always knew where she was. What she did. Even when she went into the business, much to my chagrin."

"She's no longer a child, Greta," said DeKok gently. "She's an adult woman."

"What's that got to do with it?" she snapped.

"Could she have left with Rickie?"

"I don't think so." She shook her head and looked sad. "She would have told me. Believe me. Tina had no secrets from me. And she didn't *have* to have secrets from me. She knows she can trust me."

"Maybe Rickie didn't want her to tell you?"

Greta lifted a teary face toward him.

"Rickie was afraid himself."

"Afraid," asked DeKok, startled

She nodded slowly.

"You know, DeKok," she began, "men don't have to tell me much. I know them too well. I can see by their faces, by their attitude . . . how they think, what they feel. I don't make mistakes in that department anymore." Again she shook her head, wiping away a tear. "Not me," she continued. "The last time Rickie was here he said: 'All good things must come to an end, isn't that so,

36

Greta?' I looked into his eyes and I saw fear and a great sadness. I said: 'Yes, my boy, all good things must come to an end, you're right. But that's life.' He just nodded." She fell silent for a long time, stared into the distance without seeing anything. Then she looked at DeKok.

"Rickie didn't have an easy life," she said. "I watched him leave, the last time he was here. His back, his wide shoulders . . . they were bent . . . bent as if he carried the load of the world. He looked like a man who knew the end was near."

* * *

"Nonsense." Vledder gesticulated wildly. His face was red and he looked excited. "All nonsense. No more than the sentimental maudlin of an old whore, who felt self-important because of your visit. It's all finished with Rickie because when he left his shoulders were bent." He grinned without mirth. "What sort of value can a cop assign to a statement like that? The only fact we gathered, the only concrete information is that Tina and her lover haven't been there for over a week. Well, that only confirms my point of view: They took off together."

"And that closes the case?"

Vledder nodded with emphasis.

"Or would you like to investigate a marital slip in Amsterdam, of all places?" It sounded sarcastic. "In that case you better ask the Chief Constable to recruit a few more detectives."

DeKok walked away. Slowly, dignified, calm. He knew how Vledder could get emotional, how he could passionately embrace a certain theory and how he had a tendency to approach problems in a straight-forward, uncomplicated manner. He didn't mind. The two diametrically opposed characters made a good team. The old, doubting veteran who had seen it all and the young, eager rookie who wanted to solve all the world's problems quickly and simply, preferably with the aid of technology. But police work, according to DeKok, was first, foremost and always a science of people, not machines. He stopped after a few paces and turned to Vledder.

"As soon as we're back," he said, I would like you to send out an APB. *The Commissaris of Police at Warmoes Street, Amsterdam,*" he dictated, "*requests at the behest of the family information regarding the location and whereabouts of a man, named Richard Vankerk, and a woman, named Alberdina Tuijlinga.* Then add the usual descriptions and other information and make sure they'll know that we're only suspecting an accident, not foul play, or anything like that."

"Alberdina Tuijlinga?"

"Yes," nodded DeKok. "It's Blonde Tina's real name."

* * *

It was raining and there was a strong, chill wind. The neon lights reflected in the shiny macadam of the streets while Vledder steered the police VW into the direction of the Dam, the large central square in Amsterdam.

DeKok was slouched in the passenger seat, contentedly sucking on a peppermint he had found in one of his pockets. The green light of the communication gear gave his face a ghostly appearance. Vledder turned behind the Royal Place and entered Town Hall Street, He increased his speed.

"Where are you going?" asked DeKok.

"Taking you home. It's pretty late."

DeKok shook his head decisively.

"First I want to talk to the doorman of the hotel."

Vledder shook his head in exasperation.

"What do you expect the man to tell you? That the loving couple, as usual, rented a suite?" He shrugged his shoulders. "How's that going to help us?"

"Just drop me in front of the hotel." said DeKok, not bothering to answer the question. "I'll go inside by myself."

Vledder was offended and kept his mouth shut. He stopped the car in front of the large hotel on Leiden Square.

DeKok pulled up his coat collar, pulled his hat deeper into his eyes and stepped into the rain.

The doorman, a vision in blue and gold, received him condescendingly. His attitude changed when DeKok identified himself.

"Ah, yes," said the man. "Inspector DeKok, I've heard the name. And you want information about Mr. and Mrs. Vankerk?"

DeKok nodded.

"According to my information they were here only last week."

The doorman put on his glasses and leafed through a large notebook he kept in his lodge.

"Yes," he admitted after a short search, "last Tuesday. Last Tuesday afternoon." He smiled. "They checked out at four in the afternoon."

"Were they here long?"

"A day and a night."

"You were on duty when they left?"

"Yes. I worked second shift that week. We like Mr. Vankerk very much. He's a welcome guest in the hotel and he comes often. He's usually accompanied by a blonde lady. I must say that . . ."

"That afternoon?" urged DeKok.

The man lifted his cap and scratched his skull. Then he replaced the cap and looked at DeKok.

"As I remember it, it was rather a sudden departure. He made a number of phone calls and suddenly he asked for his bill."

"Did he ever leave hurriedly before?"

"No, whether he stayed a short, or a long time, we always had plenty of warning before he left."

"Any idea who he talked to on the telephone?"

The doorman did not find it strange to be asked those questions. Like most European doormen, certainly those in the better hotels, he knew more about what was going on with individual guests than anyone else of the personnel. But this time he could not help the Inspector.

"No, I don't know," he answered. "The calls are automatic. But he *did* make an international call. Perhaps I can find out about that."

"Did he appear nervous, under tension?"

The doorman replaced his glasses in his pocket.

"In a hurry, I would say. That's the right description. He asked me to hurry and get his car, a blue Jaguar. I took care of it immediately. They had not much luggage, also not unusual. I helped the lady get in the car and he took off almost as soon as she was seated."

DeKok rubbed the back of his neck.

"Anything else unusual about the departure?"

The man smiled again.

"The tip . . . it was unusually satisfactory."

* * *

The rain splashed DeKok full in the face as he returned to the car. He opened the door of the old VW and sat down with a pensive look on his face.

"Well?" prodded Vledder tensely.

"They left in a hurry," sighed DeKok.

"That's all?"

"Yes."

Vledder turned toward his old partner.

"I just don't understand you, DeKok," he said impatiently. "This is an ordinary case. Why, in heavens' name, are you so interested in Vankerk's disappearance?"

"Perhaps," said DeKok, "because Lame Greta and I are a lot alike. We're both old, foolish and sentimental."

Vledder's mouth fell open.

"Car W1," interrupted the radio suddenly. "Car W1, report."

Vledder grabbed the microphone.

"W1, go ahead."

"W1, base. Proceed to Emperors Canal, corner Gentlemen Street."

DeKok grabbed the microphone.

"What's going on?" he demanded. "Is that you, Theo?"

The base operator gave up. Normal radio procedures went out the window when DeKok came on the air.

"That's right, DeKok," answered Theo Jansen, the constable on communications duty at Warmoes Street. "They found a man and a woman in the water next to the houseboat of a family Verwoort. And since your APB . . ."

DeKok interrupted.

"Are they holding hands?" he wanted to know.

There was a brief silence.

"That's right, DeKok," answered Theo Jansen. "The man's right hand is intertwined with the woman's left hand."

DeKok licked his dry lips. He glanced at Vledder. The young man's face was pale as he put the old car into gear.

4

DeKok watched the glistening water of the Emperors Canal from his vantage point on the bridge. There was a slight current because the canals of Amsterdam were being replenished. About every twenty four hours the waters from the extensive canal system are pumped out toward the North Sea, while fresh water from the Ijssel Lake is pumped into the system. The Ijssel Lake used to be called Zuyder Zee when it was still an inland sea, notorious for its wild storms and shallow depths resulting in the loss of many lives. DeKok's father had been a fisherman on the Zuyder Zee, but today DeKok's island was a low hill amidst fields of grain. If there's one thing the Dutch know, thought DeKok, it's how to deal with water. We drain it, we dam it, or we use it. As he thought those thoughts he was completely oblivious to the fact that the very bridge on which he was standing was at least several feet below sea level.

While a part of his mind was occupied with water, the main thrust of his attention was on the two corpses that slowly rotated in the weak current, illuminated by the spotlight from the police car on the side. The two corpses floated face down. Every once in a while the back of the man would rise slightly above the surface and then sink down again. The long, blonde hair of the woman was spread over the surface like a strange, pale seaweed.

DeKok's face was expressionless. He remembered how, not too long ago, a number of juvenile delinquents had thrown a Turkish guest worker in the water at this very same spot. The man could not swim and drowned before anyone had realized that. There was, of course, no excuse for their actions, but non-swimmers were almost unheard of in the Netherlands.

He watched as the cops of the special drown unit tried to snare the corpses with a large net. They did not have much luck. One of them looked up toward DeKok.

"Do they have to stay together?"

DeKok made a speaking trumpet of his hands.

"Hold on," he roared.

With ruthless disregard for toes, he worked his way through the crowd of curiosity seekers on the bridge and approached the house boat. He politely lifted his hat to the occupants who were standing next to their gang plank. Then he went aboard and walked toward the open stern. He placed a hand on the shoulder of one of the cops.

"There's a photographer on the way," he said. "I would like to have some pictures *before* they're separated."

The cop nodded his understanding, made a motion to his partners and eased up on the net.

DeKok squatted down and looked into the water. He could clearly see how the fingers were entwined. Frozen in death. A platinum ring with diamonds could be seen on the man's hand. Vledder breathed deeply behind him.

"Are they them?" he asked.

DeKok nodded slowly.

"I haven't had a clear view of the faces, just from the side. But I'm almost sure they are Richard Vankerk and Blonde Tina . . . together."

Vledder shook his head.

"H-how absurd," he stammered.

Bram Weelen, DeKok's favorite photographer, tapped the gray sleuth on the shoulder.

"I'm pressed for time," he said, "I hope we can do this quickly?"

DeKok rose to a standing position. He gave the photographer a scorching look.

"You're always in a hurry," he growled. "But it will take whatever time it needs."

Bram made an apologetic gesture.

"Come on, DeKok," he pleaded. "It's Louise' birthday. She's my oldest daughter and I promised to stop by."

DeKok ignored the pleading tone and the information. He pointed at the corpses.

"Does it seem familiar?"

"What do you mean?"

"Arm in arm, entwined fingers."

Bram Weelen leaned closer to the water.

"Dammit," he said, shaken, "just like the couple a few days ago." Slowly he rose, he was now pale. "Dammit," he said again, "it's starting to look like some sort of ritual." He licked dry lips. "Married too?"

"You mean, to each other?"

"Yes."

"No," said DeKok. "He's some guy with money. The woman is . . . was a prostitute."

Bram Weelen stared at the corpses, a nervous grin on his face.

"No reason to drown yourself," he said roughly, hiding his emotions.

He lowered the heavy bag from his shoulder and opened it. With quick, sure movements he selected a lens and assembled his expensive Hasselblad. He glanced at DeKok.

"I hope they come out all right. The water acts like a mirror, you know, especially at this time of night." He turned back to his case and selected a filter.

"That's your business," said DeKok, "but if the pictures aren't usable, I *will* speak harshly to you."

Weelen looked offended.

"Why so nasty? Surely I don't deserve that. Especially on my daughter's birthday."

DeKok's face softened.

"Congratulations," he smiled spontaneously. "Let's hope that we may celebrate many more birthdays with Louise."

The photographer grimaced, but gladly shook DeKok's outstretched hand.

When, in DeKok's judgement, he had taken all the pictures needed, the drown unit went back to work. It proved impossible to get both bodies out of the water at the same time without damaging them on the rough, brick sides of the canal. Eventually they managed to pry the hands loose and before long both bodies were stretched out on the stern of the houseboat. Bram Weelen went back to work and made a second series of pictures.

Vledder stared somberly at the waterlogged bodies.

"No question about it," he murmured, "it's them."

Meanwhile Weelen changed lenses yet again and finally finished. With the camera in hand and an expectant look on his face, he turned to DeKok.

"That's it for me," he said. "Unless you have special requests."

"Just a moment," said DeKok and then turned to Vledder. "Take the statements of the people who discovered the corpses," he instructed. "Thank the owners of this houseboat and check around the neighborhood. You never know. Somebody may have seen something."

"Then what?"

"Meet me back at the office."

The morgue attendants had arrived. One of them kneeled next to the corpses and pushed the arms closer to the bodies. The dead hands reached up like claws and DeKok shivered involuntarily. Those clawing hands in the harsh glare of the spotlights gave an eerie aspect to the scene on the small deck; a horrifying evidence of a suffocating death.

The other morgue attendant placed the stretcher next to the corpse of Blonde Tina. Quickly the lifeless body was placed on the stretcher, covered with a tarpaulin and carried away. They returned for the second corpse. Then the doors closed and the vehicle drove away. The curiosity seekers slowly dispersed.

DeKok watched the red lights of the morgue van disappear down the side of the canal and then he turned toward Weelen.

"Come on, old friend," he said cheerfully, "you and I aren't through yet."

* * *

In the bare, white-tiled morgue DeKok and Weelen watched with resignation as an experienced attendant quickly divested both corpses of their clothes. Sometimes it seemed as if the corpses protested, wanted to retain their dignity, but the rigid limbs were no defence against the remorseless routine. Without a trace of emotion, the attendant threw the clothes on a heap and used a hose to rinse off the bodies.

Dr. Koning, the Coroner, entered the chilly room. DeKok walked toward him and greeted him politely. Despite his old-fashioned clothes, the striped pants, the spats and the large, floppy Garibaldi hat, there was nothing ridiculous about the old doctor. He merely looked like a visitor from an earlier age.

"Yes, yes, DeKok," said the Coroner in his high, creaking voice. "I heard about it and came straight here. Apparently there is some similarity with a previous find."

DeKok nodded.

"Yes, again the arms and fingers entwined."

"Strange."

"To say the least."

"Drowning again?"

"I don't know," answered DeKok, shrugging his shoulders. "On the surface it seems that way."

"Was that a pun, DeKok?" asked the old man severely.

"No, no, certainly not, doctor," apologized DeKok hastily, "Just an unfortunate choice of words."

"Hm," grunted Dr. Koning. "Do you know who they are?"

"I know their names. They've both been missing for some time."

The Coroner looked at him.

"Any indications of suicide?"

"None."

Dr. Koning removed his large, greenish Garibaldi hat and leaned over the corpse of Blonde Tina. DeKok motioned to Weelen.

"I want a close-up of every square inch of their skins," he instructed the photographer.

"What do you expect to find?"

"Nothing," growled DeKok, irked, "nothing sensible."

Bram Weelen shrugged his shoulders and went to work.

Dr. Koning motioned to the attendant and the man rolled Blonde Tina's corpse face up. DeKok was surprised to see how little the body seemed to have suffered from its immersion in the water.

The Coroner pushed forcefully on the rib-cage and canal water bubbled from the mouth. Dr. Koning made a sad, apologetic gesture as he looked at DeKok.

"It seems they may have drowned, after all," he allowed.

DeKok did not react. He had expected it more or less, but in his heart he was not satisfied. He could not rid himself of the feeling that he was missing something as if the bodies were telling him something in a language he did not understand.

Dr. Koning followed the same procedure with Richard Vankerk's corpse. He also looked at every part of the skin. The flashes from Weelen's Hasselblad did not seem to bother him in the least. When water bubbled from Vankerk's mouth as well, after Dr. Koning had pressed on the man's rib-cage, DeKok looked mystified.

"But that's impossible," he exclaimed. "There has to be an explanation. Nobody commits suicide this way. Nobody. I've never even *heard* of such a thing, let alone experienced it."

The old Coroner cleaned his pince-nez on a sleeve of his old-fashioned coat.

"They are dead," he announced solemnly.

DeKok looked down at the old man.

"Drowned, I presume?"

"I'm sorry," said the old doctor, "I don't want to be precipitous, that's to say, I don't want to anticipate the official autopsy, but . . . yes, it looks that way."

He replaced his old hat and with a condescending nod at those present, he left.

DeKok watched him leave. For a few seconds he seemed undecided. Then he looked at his watch. He hastily stuffed the wet clothes in a plastic bag. He hoisted the bag on his shoulder and ran out of the room. Bram Weelen watched with open mouth. DeKok at speed was a comical sight and the large bag bobbing on his shoulder made him look like an ungainly Santa

49

Claus in mufti. Hastily Weelen packed his equipment and ran after the fast disappearing DeKok.

"Where are you going?" he panted as he caught up with the gray sleuth.

DeKok slowed down and turned toward him, a broad smile on his face.

"To Louise, your daughter. We have exactly twenty minutes left to congratulate her with her birthday *on* her birthday."

* * *

Young Vledder shook his head regretfully.

"Nothing . . . not a peep. I visited all the occupied houses in the neighborhood and checked with all the houseboats on that stretch of the canal. Most people remembered the tragic death of the Turk, but nobody could tell me anything about this case." He leaned on his desk. "About when could they have drowned?"

"On, or about the first of the month. Nobody has seen them since they left the hotel on Tuesday."

Vledder nodded thoughtfully.

"Last night, when I came back, I put through an APB on the blue Jaguar. I wonder where it'll be found. It's got to be somewhere."

"Perhaps," sighed DeKok, "and perhaps it will help us, but I fear the worst." He stared into the distance, an angry look on his face. "We're dealing with a very clever, a very cunning opponent."

"So you're convinced it's murder?"

"Without a shadow of a doubt."

"But why . . . I mean . . . what's the motive?"

DeKok pointed at the long table on which the contents of Vankerk's wallet were drying out.

"Anything that could give us the smallest lead has been removed."

Vledder's eyes widened.

"And the money?"

"What money?"

"I checked with the bank. On the first of February Richard Vankerk took a little over a hundred thousand in cash from his account."

"That's quite a sum." whistled DeKok.

"He had a private account with ABN, Algemene Bank Nederland, and he cleaned it out."

DeKok pointed at the table.

"As you can see: no money."

"Robbery, murder with robbery?"

"I wish it were that simple," said DeKok. Then he shook his head. "But I don't believe it. There's a deeper, darker mystery behind the secret of the drownings."

Vledder gave him a penetrating look.

"Drownings? Plural? You think there's a connection between Tina and Vankerk and the Shoebeek couple?"

"Absolutely."

Vledder grimaced.

"You don't think somebody could be imitating the original deaths? I mean, whoever killed Vankerk and Blonde Tina could have just taken the Shoebeek's death as an example, as a model. It could have given him ideas."

DeKok shook his head.

"That's impossible."

"Why?" asked Vledder, surprised.

"It takes a while before drowned corpses start to float," answered DeKok. "When the Shoebeeks were fished from the water, Vankerk and Tina were already dead."

The phone rang. Vledder picked it up and listened. After a few minutes he replaced the receiver.

"It's for you," he said hoarsely. "It's the doorman from the hotel. He checked the international call made by Vankerk."

"And?"

"The call was to Cortina d'Ampezzo."

5

Commissaris Buitendam, the tall, stately chief of Warmoes Street Station, motioned with an elegant, well-manicured, somewhat effeminate hand.

"Come in, DeKok," he said in his cultured, affected voice.

DeKok stared at him, not for the first time wondering what mischievous imp had been responsible for assigning the aristocratic man to be in charge of the hurly-burly of the busy station. DeKok had no quarrel with the man's rank. And he could certainly see him in charge of some administrative department at Headquarters, or even as a seasoned diplomat in one of the more civilized capitals of the world. He would be eminently suited for either. But in Warmoes Street, of all places, among whores, pimps, drunks and a wide collection of criminals ranging from petty thieves to drug runners and murderers, Commissaris Buitendam was out of his element. It was a pity that so few people seemed to be aware of it, least of all the man himself.

"If it's all the same to you," answered the gray sleuth, "I'd rather stand."

The Commissaris moved uneasily in his chair.

"As you will." Buitendam coughed discreetly. "I have," he continued pompously, "conveyed your urgent request for a judicial autopsy on the remains of Richard Vankerk and Alberdina Tuijlinga to the Judge-Advocate."

"And?" DeKok looked tense.

The Commissaris coughed again.

"It is the considered opinion of the Judge-Advocate," he answered hesitantly, "that there are few reasons to suspect foul play to be a factor in the unfortunate demise of the named individuals. Also, in view of the Coroner's opinion, the Judge-Advocate is reluctant to accept any other cause of death, other than simple drowning as a result of a double suicide."

DeKok gestured violently.

"What nonsense is this?" he demanded heatedly. "What is a 'simple' drowning? For all we know somebody held their heads under water until they drowned. And what would the Judge-Advocate call that? A 'simple' drowning, or murder?"

The usually pale face of the Commissaris reddened. He leaned forward.

"Are there any indications that the victims were held under water?"

DeKok felt the anger inside himself and controlled it with an effort.

"There are also no indications that it did *not* happen," he bristled. He shook his gray head and snorted contemptuously. "What's the matter with the Judge-Advocate? Does he have blinders on? Or is the workload getting too much for him?"

The Commissaris stood up.

"I forbid you," he said seriously, "to express yourself in that manner regarding your superiors."

DeKok pressed his lips together. He seemed ready to explode. Then he spoke in a surprisingly mild tone of voice which somehow, seemed all the more threatening to his chief.

"I know no superiors," said DeKok. "I do know," he added reasonably, "a few people who, through no credit of their own,

54

happen to temporarily fill a higher function in the pecking order than mine."

The Commissaris leaned closer, ignoring the sarcasm.

"In that case you should respect their decisions," he admonished.

DeKok grinned defiantly.

"Respect?" he asked, a jeering tone in his voice, "respect? How can I possibly respect a wrong decision? The case of these double drownings stinks . . . . stinks to high heaven and believe me, it's not just the smell of the canal water from which we fished the corpses." He took a deep breath. "And I'll prove it, despite a Judge-Advocate who fails to see his duty."

The Commissaris would take no more. His eyes spat fire and he stretched a trembling finger toward the door.

"OUT!" he roared.

DeKok left.

* * *

Vledder laughed at him when he returned to the detective room.

"Same story again?" asked the young man. "You must be nice to the Commissaris. I have told you before. How do they state that in the regulations? You must be polite and helpful to the public and you must be polite and respectful to your . . . eh, to those placed over you." Vledder knew all about DeKok's opinion on superiors. The old man was a confirmed egalitarian. "Anyway, he concluded, *polite* is the operative word."

DeKok grinned, unable to nurse his anger.

"Regulations," he mocked. "According to the regulations, my so-called job description, I'm being paid to prevent and solve crimes. That's the reason they pay me . . . and I don't take it kindly when some Judge-Advocate tries to prevent me from doing my duty."

Young Vledder shook his head.

"But the man is not trying to prevent you from anything . . . he just has a different view of it all, no more. Surely, that's allowed?"

DeKok's face had again the mild expression of a good-natured boxer. His anger had abated.

"Of course, that's allowed," he admitted readily. "Besides, I really don't know if an autopsy will show anything else than that the victims did indeed drown."

"In other words, it might not help us at all."

DeKok looked pensively over Vledder's head.

"It's an open question. More than likely you're right and it won't help at all. You see, drowning is never simple, neither as a suicide, or as murder. It's a known fact that a swimmer seldom chooses death by drowning. The body will always fight the mind."

"Could the victims swim?"

"I don't know that either," shrugged DeKok. "I *do* know that Tina was a pretty good swimmer. She used to be a member of a swim club and used to compete . . . quite creditably."

"And with murder . . . what are the possibilities?"

DeKok gestured vaguely.

"It's not easy to keep someone under water against their will. There will always be a struggle, especially since the victim, in extremis, so to speak, often commands super-human powers."

The young Inspector nodded thoughtfully.

"And that might lead to marks on the body . . . also, there were *two* victims at a time. That might indicate more than one perpetrator."

DeKok rubbed the bridge of his nose with a little finger. Then he stared at it for some time. Finally he lowered his finger and used it to rummage in his breast pocket. With an expression of triumph he found a dusty peppermint. He wiped it off and popped it in his mouth.

"Or the killer had a technical advantage," said DeKok after a long pause.

"Technical?" questioned Vledder.

"Yes, he, or she, might have been wearing a diving suit, one of those self-contained ones, you know."

"A scuba suit?"

"Yes, whatever they call them."

Vledder, always ready to embrace a workable theory and pursue it with single-minded enthusiasm, looked happy.

"That's it," he exclaimed. "A diving suit." Then his face sobered. "But that raises another question: Why would someone be diving in the canals, especially in February?" He shook his head sadly. "It remains a mystery ... a strange set of circumstances. I just don't see a solution. It's just too crazy for words." He looked at DeKok. "I think this one has us stumped."

DeKok winked at him.

"Come, come, we're cops, after all. We're supposed to have all the answers, even if we don't have all the questions yet."

Vledder smiled.

"Did we find out who Richard Vankerk talked to internationally?"

"You mean the call to Cortina?"

"Yes."

DeKok pushed his lower lip forward. Then he took the peppermint out of his mouth and inspected its progress. He replaced it on his tongue and leaned forward.

"I had hoped that Richard had talked to the Shoebeeks. Perhaps we could have found some connection between the two double murders." He scratched the back of his neck. "I would have had a stronger case to present to the Old Man."

"And?"

"At the time when Richard Vankerk was talking to Cortina d'Ampezzo, the Shoebeeks were already back in Holland."

"So, *who* did he talk to?" wondered Vledder.

DeKok shrugged his shoulders.

"He talked to a hotel. According to the available information he had a nine-minute conversation with someone in the Albergo Cristallo on Viale Bernini."

"Where's that?"

"In Cortina," said DeKok, irritated, "what else were we talking about?"

"Sorry," said Vledder, "I meant *what* is it . . . what sort of hotel?"

"I see what you mean," said DeKok, mollified. "It's a large, fancy hotel just outside Cortina."

"And the Shoebeeks didn't stay there?"

"No," grinned DeKok. "I thought you were going to ask something different. The Shoebeeks are . . . proper, middle-class people, with middle class incomes."

"And the Cristallo was too expensive for them . . . I see. What did you think I was going to ask?"

"Who stayed there . . . but that's probably impossible to find out. Besides, a hotel like that has a lot of public phones. Anybody could have used them."

"Oh." Vledder looked puzzled. "Still," he continued, "it seems such a coincidence. The Shoebeeks, after returning from a vacation in Cortina, are fished from the canals . . . and the same thing happens to Vankerk and Blonde Tina, after he talks to Cortina."

"And you feel there's a connection?"

"Yes, no, I don't know . . . something."

DeKok remained silent and Vledder could hear distinctly as he crunched the last of his peppermint. Suddenly DeKok went to the coat rack and grabbed his raincoat and his ubiquitous little felt hat.

"Let's go," he said to Vledder.

"Where?" asked Vledder as he slowly rose from behind his desk.

"To Oldwater on the Amstel."

"Why are we going there?"

"We're going to visit a lady . . . a Rosita Stuyvenberg."

"And who, pray tell, is Rosita Stuyvenberg?"

"The ex-wife of Richard Vankerk. She lives on Round Hoop in Oldwater . . . she and two grown sons."

* * *

They drove along the Amstel, after which Amsterdam was named, as the river snaked its way through the surrounding low lands. Amsterdam had originated as a dam across the Amstel, soon houses and streets were added. Warmoes Street, where DeKok and Vledder were based, is the oldest street in Amsterdam.

The surface of the water was almost level with the roadbed. DeKok looked around. A low, gray cloud cover seemed to rob the surroundings of color and created an eerie, misty light. He pulled up his collar and slumped down in the seat.

The two double drownings bothered him and not just because the Judge-Advocate had resisted all arguments for an autopsy. The entire affair seemed so senseless, so completely without motive. It was impossible to come to a conclusion on the meager facts available. Those involved had little, if anything, in common. The Shoebeeks were a rather colorless couple. What could possibly possess the perpetrator to seek their life in such an emphatic way? He grinned sadly to himself. Or was the Judge-Advocate correct? Was it really no more than suicide?

He thought he knew enough about Blonde Tina's background. A young hooker from the District. But there were few surprises there, too. The only one of the four who had some substance, stood out, was Richard Vankerk. How old was he when he died? At least half a century. What had he done, accomplished, during that period? How did he get his money? What was the purpose of the large sum of money he took from the bank, shortly before his death? What did he need the money for? And . . . perhaps more important . . . what had happened to the money? His sad grin changed into a confident smile. It would be worth his while to do a little digging into the life of Richard Vankerk.

Vledder glanced at him from the side.

"Private joke?"

DeKok pulled himself up.

"Unattractive women are *always* jealous of their husbands, beautiful women are never jealous. It's something Oscar Wilde is supposed to have said."

"And what is that supposed to mean?" asked Vledder, surprise in his voice.

DeKok smiled thinly.

"I haven't seen Rosita Stuyvenberg yet."

* * *

They took the bridge across the Amstel and after passing the traffic light they entered the narrow main street of Oldwater. To the left was the ancient Town Hall. DeKok gazed at it wistfully. Time, he considered, was an illusion. Everything you tried to retain, would inevitably slip through your fingers. But then again, he smiled to himself, was time something that should be frozen, kept static? No, he decided, time was to be used, to be lived, concisely, intensely. He looked at the white-washed

60

building. It held tender memories for him. It was here, more than twenty-five years ago, that he had married his wife. He still considered it the smartest thing he had ever done in his life.

Past Town Hall they turned right in the direction of the Jewish Cemetery and from there around the Protestant Cross Church. An alley, hardly wider than the VW, led to a wooden draw bridge. DeKok looked back as they crossed the old bridge. Except for the cars and the electric street lights, Oldwater looked as it had looked for the last few centuries. Round Hoop was outside the core of the ancient little town, on the other side of the Amstel. The narrow Amstel Dike eventually split off into a modern, wide street.

Vledder reduced speed and turned into a driveway. The gravel crunched under the tires of the car. DeKok looked at the stately house that was revealed at the end of the long driveway. A hedge of conifers surrounded an immense garden.

"This it?"

Vledder double-checked his note book.

"This is the address you gave me."

"Impressive. Apparently Richard Vankerk was able to provide his ex-wife with substantial alimony."

"Perhaps Rosita has her own capital," shrugged Vledder.

They left the car and walked toward the front door. An intricately wrought door knocker was attached to one side. DeKok pulled at the ring that was held by a brass lion's mouth and they heard a bell ring inside the house.

It took several minutes and then the heavy door opened slowly. A tall, distinguished woman stood on the threshold. DeKok thought she might be in her late forties. She wore a dark-blue, almost black dress and a beautiful, silver pendant on a chain around her neck. Her dark hair had been pulled back tightly and ended in a chignon. She looked with surprise at the two men and raised her eyebrows in a questioning gesture.

The gray sleuth lifted his head and bowed slightly.

"My name is DeKok," he said in a friendly tone of voice. He waved aside. "My colleague, Vledder. We are police inspectors, attached to Warmoes Street station in Amsterdam."

She was obviously confused. She cocked her head, inviting further explanation.

"Amsterdam?" she asked.

"Yes," nodded DeKok. "And you are Rosita Stuyvenberg?"

"Indeed."

DeKok made a shy gesture.

"We . . . eh, we wanted to talk to you. We wanted to discuss the sudden demise of your . . . eh, your ex-husband, Richard Vankerk." He paused, looked at her. "I presume you have been informed?" he asked.

She seemed to stand straighter.

"I have been told." He tone was cool and business-like.

DeKok hesitated. Then he plunged on.

"I can understand that the subject is not . . . is not, eh, a pleasant one, but . . ."

She interrupted him with an imperial gesture of one hand and opened the door wider.

"Please come in."

She locked the door carefully after they had entered and then preceded them to a high, spacious room with exquisite tapestries on the walls. She made an inviting gesture in the direction of some easy chairs.

"Please sit down."

DeKok studied the room surreptitiously. The room was sparsely, but exquisitely furnished. Across from the tapestries the entire wall was covered with bookcases and DeKok saw a number of venerable, leather bindings.

"I understand that Richard could no longer endure life."

62

She had taken a seat across from the Inspectors, stiff, straight, with her knees close together. DeKok nodded to himself, a serious expression on his face.

"You mean . . . that he committed suicide?"

She looked at him, a weary look in her eyes.

"Isn't that what happened?"

DeKok did not answer at once. He scratched the tip of his nose with a little finger and then was lost for several seconds while he contemplated the digit.

"Do you have any reason," he asked carefully, after a long pause, ". . . to suspect that your ex-husband was capable of such a desperate act?"

Rosita Stuyvenberg remained silent and lowered her head.

DeKok took the opportunity to study her in detail. She still had a good figure, he concluded. The tight dress did nothing to hide that. The oval face with the ivory skin had a quiet beauty all its own. She raised her head to meet his gaze.

"Richard had an admirable knack for getting into trouble."

DeKok listened to the tone of voice. There was an undercurrent of hate, mockery and contempt.

"What sort of trouble?"

She looked evenly at DeKok.

"Women."

DeKok nodded his understanding.

"He left you at the time for Monique . . ."

She interrupted him vehemently.

"Left me?" she asked sharply. "Left me? He did not leave *me*. I simply sent him away. I had had it up to here with his affairs."

DeKok allowed his gaze to wander around the room.

"At least . . . he did not leave you wanting," he said.

Rosita Stuyvenberg laughed scornfully.

"Thank God, I have never had to rely on him for financial support. Even after the divorce I refused to accept a penny from him. Not even child support."

DeKok looked at her sadly.

"You're still angry," he concluded.

She hesitated before she answered. She leaned forward and placed her hands on her knees.

"That . . . that Monique became his Nemesis."

"Nemesis?"

"Yes, in my place . . . she became my Adrastea, my goddess of divine retribution . . . she treated him the way he treated me."

"She was unfaithful?"

"Unfaithful?" She smiled. ""Unfaithful? It was much worse than that. She destroyed his male pride and humiliated him to such an extent that he looked for solace with girls from the street, with whores."

DeKok rubbed his chin.

"You're well informed," he said with admiration in his voice.

A shadow fled across her handsome face. Her expression changed to one of sadness, almost melancholy.

"After all . . . he is, was the father of my two sons," she said softly. Suddenly she pressed her lips together and her eyes narrowed. "and if I discover," she hissed, "any of his characteristics in either one of them, I'll . . ."

A young man entered the room and she stopped talking. DeKok estimated him to be in his late twenties. He wore an expensive, well-cut dark suit, a white shirt and a subdued tie. He carried himself proudly and had the open face of a man driven by certainties, aware of his own worth.

Rosita Stuyvenberg stood up and greeted the young man with a kiss. She took him by an arm and presented him to the two cops.

"Alfred Vankerk," she said with pride, "my older son."

Vledder and DeKok rose and pressed the outstretched hand.

"Brother Constantin," warbled the young man.

Rosita gestured.

"These are Inspectors from the police station at Warmoes Street in Amsterdam. They're here in connection with the death of your father."

The young man's face became rigid. He lifted an arm in a dramatic gesture.

"The Evil One has done his work," he declared loudly. "Chained to the object of his sins . . .. he descends into the bottomless pit."

6

They drove back to Amsterdam at a sedate pace. Vledder stared at the road. His face showed he was deep in thought.

"So," he said somberly, "Alfred Vankerk is also a member of the Community of the Brothers and Sisters of the Holy Blessings."

DeKok rubbed the back of his neck.

"Where he's known as Brother Constantin."

The young Inspector shook his head, confused.

"You've got to admit it's a strange case. Sort of tantalizingly mysterious. I can't make head nor tail out of it." He sighed deeply. "It simply *cannot* be mere coincidence that the Shoebeeks belonged to the same group."

"And died in the same way."

Vledder negotiated a narrow, sharp turn. When the road straightened out again, he glanced aside.

"I," he said formally, "am beginning to believe in murder as well."

DeKok grinned amiably.

"Better late than never. I'm glad you're starting to trust your instincts."

"Mind you," answered Vledder, trying to deny he was going by instinct, "I was tempted to make an exception for the Shoebeeks."

"You really saw that as a double suicide?" DeKok asked, while he put a toffee in his mouth.

"Yes, I did," asserted Vledder. "But," he added, "the two cases are too identical. Richard Vankerk's death and that of Tina ... there are too many similarities. That's more than just coincidence."

DeKok nodded agreement.

"What's your opinion of Rosita?" he queried.

Vledder looked pained.

"That's hard to say. On the surface she seems cool, collected, almost disinterested. And yet, she can hardly hide her feelings of hate for her ex-husband."

DeKok rubbed his chin.

"I wonder how much of that hate has been an influence on the children." He looked at Vledder. "And what about Brother Constantin?"

"Just as fanatical, smug and holier-than-thou as that Brother Crispin who visited us at the station."

"Did you listen to what he said?"

"Who?"

"Constantin."

"The Evil One has done his work," laughed Vledder.

"Exactly ... and what else?"

"Marked by ..." Vledder hesitated. "No, that wasn't it. Wait ... I got it ... 'Chained to the object of his sins he descends into the bottomless pit.' That's it." He looked at DeKok for confirmation.

DeKok pursed his lips and nodded thoughtfully.

"A strange thing to say," added Vledder, "Especially for a son who's talking about the death of his own father."

The gray sleuth moved the toffee behind his teeth.

"But, when looked at in the light of a religious fanatic . . . quite understandable. In those circles that sort of tone and that kind of expression are common fare." He raised a finger in the air. "But let us dissect the thoughts behind such a remark. Who was the object of his sins?"

"Blonde Tina, of course, the whore."

"Excellent, really excellent. And what is meant by *chained*."

"Together . . . attached to each other."

DeKok pushed his hat further back on his head.

"In other words . . . what Brother Constantin said . . . was that his father died while attached to Blonde Tina, arm in arm, fingers entwined . . . chained together, so to speak."

"Yes, well, so what?"

DeKok swallowed the last piece of his toffee with a look of regret.

"How," he asked, "did Brother Constantin know that the bodies of his father and Tina were found that way? I purposely kept that little detail from the papers. It's just not widely known."

Vledder swallowed.

"But . . . but that means . . ."

"Exactly," beamed DeKok. "It means that our Brother Constantin may have said more than he wanted us to know."

* * *

There was a large puddle of blood on the granite floor of the Pathology Laboratory in the bowels of the old Wilhelmina Hospital. The blood dripped from a stretcher where the horribly mutilated corpse of a young woman was barely covered by a rough scrap of canvas. Another victim of modern traffic. DeKok looked at the corpse. His attention seemed focused by the steadily dripping blood. Thoughtfully he noticed how the puddle gradually increased in size.

An attendant, Walk-Man in his ears, pushed the victim into a refrigerated drawer and took a hose to rinse away the blood. It drained through a grate in the floor.

DeKok hated Pathology Labs and autopsies. He avoided them as much as possible, especially when the proceedings were in the old Wilhelmina Hospital. The underground spaces in the old building always reminded him of dungeons. The corpses in the Pathology department only reinforced that impression.

Usually he left such details to Vledder, but this time he wanted to be on hand himself. He had sent Vledder to pick up Lame Greta for the official identification of the young prostitute. He had also asked Sister Emilia of the Salvation Army to attend. The good Sister had known Tina well and the Law required two independent witnesses.

From experience DeKok knew that most people were unable to confront the victims of a violent death and he had witnessed more heartbreaking scenes than he cared to remember.

He was not too worried about Sister Emilia. She was a strong woman with a nursing background, hardened by life, but without having lost her compassionate nature. Lame Greta worried him, however. Like most prostitutes she was sentimental and highly emotional. Her behavior was difficult to predict and he hoped for the support of the Salvation Army soldier.

He watched while the attendant wheeled Tina's corpse to the center of the room and covered it with a sheet. The body looked peaceful. Except for a slight bloating of the attractive body, it might have been a young woman sunbathing in the nude. Until one noticed the pallor of the skin and the absence of any movement.

As the morgue attendant finished with Tina, DeKok looked into the waiting room. Sister Emilia stared straight in front of her, a resigned look on her face. Lame Greta was almost lost on the wide bench, a small, fragile little bird. At such moments DeKok envied pastors and priests who, on such occasions, always seemed to be able to find the right words.

From the corner of his eye DeKok caught the ready sign of the attendant and he walked into the waiting room. Gently he accompanied the two women to the black curtain and softly he pushed it aside. Only Tina's head protruded from beneath the sheet that covered her. Now that the sheet covered her, she looked more beautiful than before. Somebody had brushed her hair and the eyes were closed. She showed a pale, but healthy face. DeKok wondered who had brushed the hair. The same man who had just aimed a hose at the life-blood of what had once been another young woman?

For some time they stared in silence at the dead face. DeKok kept an eye on Lame Greta and prepared himself for the reaction that was bound to follow. He saw her lips move, but there was no sound. He leaned closer and then she suddenly spoke in a normal, soft voice:

"You must never challenge a man. You just don't."

She fell silent. Her hand reached out toward the corpse. Then it stopped. Slowly, still shaking, she withdrew her hand.

DeKok motioned with his head to the attendant. He closed the black curtain. Both women were crying. DeKok took them by the arm and led them back outside the building. Vledder was waiting in front of the building. He opened the door of the VW for the two women and then drove off after they were seated. DeKok looked at his watch. Another half hour until the next identification.

He watched the VW disappear and then took a little stroll among the flowers and plants of the old hospital. He hoped everything would go as planned. Vledder was to pick up Monique Vankerk as soon as he had dropped off the Sister and

Greta. Meanwhile Fred Prins, a young Inspector who was rapidly replacing Robert Antoine Dijk who had retired from the force, was in the process of picking up Rosita Stuyvenberg from Oldwater. She had agreed to participate in the legal identification of the deceased. Of course, DeKok had "forgotten" to tell either one of the women that he had secured the cooperation of the other.

The wily old fox grinned softly to himself. He expected a dramatic scene when the ex-wife and the widow of the late Richard Vankerk confronted each other near the corpse. In truth, he admitted to himself, it was a devilish arrangement and he wondered what exactly he expected to happen, what would be the result. Murder was a secretive and emotional business. DeKok felt that this time he was justified in bending the ethical rules slightly in order to arouse the emotions. There was still too much of a mystery surrounding the two double murders. He had to lift the veil, penetrate the fog of misdirection and . . . catch the culprits. That is what they paid him for.

Although he was still at a loss as to where to look for the guilty, he was convinced that the key was somewhere in the life of Richard Vankerk. Both Rosita and Monique had played a large role in that life. Had Tina been caught up in the chain of events, or had she also played a role. What had caused Richard to stumble? What was the reason for his demise? What sort of traps had been set by the women in his life?

DeKok shook his head sadly. He just could not arrive at a satisfactory conclusion. There were too many gaps, too many uncertainties. For instance, he reminded himself, where was the connection with the Shoebeeks? Why were they dead? Why did they have to die?

He looked at his watch again. Slowly he made his way back to the Pathology department. Before he reached the entrance to the hospital, he saw a car stop outside the gate. DeKok hastened over and held the door.

Rosita Stuyvenberg emerged. She wore a black, Persian fur coat and a matching hat. The gray sleuth greeted her heartily and led her to the waiting room outside the morgue. He took Inspector Prins aside and instructed him to stay with the woman until Vledder had arrived with Monique. Then he walked into the lab and left the door ajar.

The attendant had already placed Richard's corpse on a stretcher. He was still fiddling with the sheet. He looked up as DeKok entered.

"When are these two going to be buried?" he asked.

"I don't know exactly." DeKok shrugged his shoulders. "There's no official word. But possibly day after tomorrow, at Sorrow Field. I heard the stepmother of the girl say something like that."

The attendant tucked the sheet under Vankerk's shoulders. "You'll let me know?"

DeKok nodded.

Through the partially open door he saw Monique enter the waiting room, closely followed by Vledder. She was visibly shocked as soon as she saw Rosita Stuyvenberg. For just a moment it looked as if she was going to bolt, but after a short hesitation she proceeded further into the room and sat down as far away from Rosita as possible.

DeKok studied the two women a little longer. They were completely different. Rosita's beauty was of a different kind. She lacked the abundant, lavish attractiveness of Monique, but she possessed a clear, distinctive serenity that had an ageless quality.

Monique appeared tense, unsure of herself. She wore a wide, black coat with a frivolous beret. She moved uneasily on the hard, uncomfortable bench. She was obviously ill at ease.

DeKok made an entrance. With a winning smile on his face he approached the women and bowed formally.

"Thank you very much for coming," he said pleasantly. He looked from one to the other. "I take it I do not need to introduce you two to each other?"

There was a slight taunt in his voice.

The women did not react.

DeKok asked them to follow him. Almost by accident, he brought them closer together as he led them into the morgue room. They were almost side by side as they faced the black curtain and DeKok motioned to the attendant.

Unlike Tina, Richard Vankerk had changed in death and looked like a shadow of his former self. The skin had dried out and a gray stubble covered his face. Richard's death mask was more fearful than that of Tina.

From under his eyebrows DeKok watched the two women. Rosita Stuyvenberg looked outwardly unaffected, but DeKok thought he saw a barely controlled passion in her eyes.

Monique was pale as a ghost. Small beads of sweat pearled on her forehead. DeKok came closer to her, afraid she would collapse. But she remained standing, rigidly, as if frozen in place.

Silently they looked at the dead face. For several minutes nobody moved, or said anything. DeKok was getting restless. He had not arranged this confrontation on a whim. He wanted a reaction . . . no matter what. It took too long and he could not prolong the proceedings indefinitely.

Next to him he heard the quick, shallow breathing of Monique. He looked at her. Her face was empty, without expression, almost lifeless. Rosita looked unaffected with the same expressionless face, but now there was a slight tic at one corner of her mouth. Carefully, with drooping shoulders, DeKok took a step forward and leaned over the corpse.

"I believe," he said solemnly, "that Richard must have suffered much." His hand hovered above the face of the dead man. "Even in death his face speaks of sorrow . . . a deep sorrow."

DeKok stepped back, cursing himself silently, angry with himself for the banal words, the inept, theatrical gestures.

Tensely he waited. Perhaps there would be a reaction after all, perhaps his words had penetrated in a way he could not predict. Much to his surprise he suddenly noticed that not Monique, but Rosita was in the process of losing her self-control. Her head shook left to right and her lips quivered. With an abrupt movement she turned toward Monique.

"You," she screamed, "you killed him . . . you murdered him!" Hate flashed in her eyes. "You'll be sorry for that . . . you'll suffer for that."

7

Inspector Vledder looked at his old mentor and smiled.

"You know, DeKok," he chided, "when those women refused to react in front of Vankerk's corpse, I felt sorry for you."

"Why feel sorry? I tried to shake loose some emotions . . . force them out in the open."

"But you had expected more?"

DeKok shrugged his shoulders nonchalantly.

"Ach," he said with a sigh, "the reaction still has to come. It's pretty obvious that neither of the women has been exactly open with us. On the contrary, I'd say. And I can't help but wonder why? I can only guess at the answer. Just possibly both are more closely connected to Vankerk's murder than we suspect at the moment."

"How?"

The gray sleuth grinned broadly.

"If I knew that, we'd be a lot nearer to the solution."

Vledder pushed his chair closer, straddled it and rested his arms and head on the back of the chair.

"But Rosita accused Monique quite openly. There was no question about *that*. You killed him, she said."

"And she told her she would suffer for it."

Vledder nodded.

"An obvious threat."

DeKok placed his legs on the desk.

"Eventually we'll have to ask Rosita what exactly she meant by that remark. Perhaps I was wrong, but it seemed neither the time, nor the place, to ask her in the cold basement of the morgue. We'll have to wait for the right opportunity. Anyway . . . for what it's worth, I think we would be better off to first approach Monique. She has been lying to us from the start . . . deliberately tried to give us the wrong impression of the situation."

"You mean," said Vledder, looking at his older partner, "when she first came to report her husband missing?"

DeKok nodded thoughtfully.

"She pretended that everything was just peachy. As if she and Richard made the perfect couple. Now we know that, to say the least, she was presenting us with a view through rose-colored glasses . . . there were a few shortcomings in the relationship." He grinned. "When you asked her if there might perhaps be another woman involved, she became downright indignant and rejected the possibility out of hand . . . yet, I must assume that Richard's relationship with Blonde Tina was no secret to her. Both acted too openly for that. Also, if we can believe Lame Greta, Monique, by her . . . eh, unapproachable behavior has probably been the cause . . ." The gray sleuth stopped talking, did not complete the sentence. He lifted his legs from the desk and ambled over to the coat rack.

Vledder looked at him with amazement.

"Where on earth are you going, all of a sudden?"

DeKok motioned him closer.

"We're going back to Stove Alley . . . back to Lame Greta. She said something during the identification."

"What?"

With his little hat raised halfway to his head, DeKok stared into the distance.

"*You must never challenge a man. You just don't.*"

* * *

Lame Greta looked at DeKok and shook her head.

"That's right, you shouldn't. That is something a working girl should never do."

"But Tina did?"

"Yes."

"How?"

"Ach," she sighed resignedly, "what's the use of talking about it. Tina is dead."

DeKok gave her a sharp look.

"I cannot bring her back to life. Nobody can do that. But I *can* find her killer."

Lame Greta lowered her head.

"What do I care about the killer?"

DeKok placed his hand under her chin and gently lifted her head until he could look in her eyes.

"But I care, Greta," he said in a compelling tone of voice. "I care very much about the killer. You might say that I am obsessed with him, or her. I'm a cop. It is my *duty* to find him."

She shook her head sadly.

"I've always been like a mother to her. That's how she looked at me, treated me . . . as her mother, her only true mother. You know I never wanted her to go into the Life. I fought against it, argued with her. But Tina loved nice things."

"And Uncle Rickie had a lot of money."

Greta made a repudiating gesture.

"It wasn't that," she reacted, annoyed. "I mean, it wasn't *just* that. Tina wanted more." She looked at the gray cop, without avoiding his eyes. "You know what the girls say among each other: *Never marry a guy who visits the whores.* Tina didn't listen. She had different ideas . . . very different. She wanted to become *respectable*. She wanted to become Mrs. Vankerk. It sounds good, doesn't it? *Missus* Vankerk."

Lame Greta sounded bitter.

DeKok closed his eyes momentarily, as if in pain.

"She wanted to *marry* him?" he asked disbelief in his voice.

Greta bowed her head and nodded.

"Marry, yes . . . exactly, complete with a Marriage License and a choir in the church."

DeKok cocked his head at her.

"Is that what you meant by *challenging*?"

She sighed deeply.

"Rickie always said that he loved her very much . . . that he never in his life had loved a woman so much. And Tina would say: 'If you love me, marry me.' You see, she challenged him . . . she dared him to prove his love. And she kept on about it." Greta looked at him with a melancholy face. "I tried to tell her not to do it. I warned her over and over again. 'Don't do it,' I said, 'you'll do nothing but cause trouble for that man. It'll end badly.' But she wouldn't listen."

"How did Rickie react?"

"At last he promised Tina he would get a divorce. And as far as I know he was working on it."

"Did his wife know about Tina?"

Greta grimaced.

"He said that he had discussed Tina with her."

"And?"

"His wife apparently was not completely against a divorce. In fact, it was a marriage in name only. As far as she was concerned he had already ceased to exist. But Rickie was obviously upset about the demands she made before agreeing to a divorce."

"Financial?"

"That too," she nodded.

DeKok gave her a searching look.

"What more could there be?"

"Rickie had to resign his high position."

"What high position."

"In his Faith."

The gray sleuth leaned closer.

"Faith?" he asked. "What sort of Faith?"

She made a hesitating gesture with an unsteady hand.

"For a long time Rickie has been a member of a Community, a religious group. He did a lot of work for them."

DeKok's eyes widened.

"The Brothers and Sisters," he said tensely.

Lame Greta nodded slowly in agreement.

"Of the Holy Blessings."

* * *

They walked away from Lame Greta's house, through Old Acquaintance Alley, toward Old Church Square. They were silent. The discovery that Richard Vankerk, too, had been a member of the Brothers and Sisters of the Holy Blessings had shocked them. It suddenly gave the case a totally different twist. A whole new series of questions were rising to the surface.

At the corner of Old Church Square and St. Anna Street they encountered Limburger Lena. Lena was an older prostitute and she and DeKok seemed to have known each other all their lives. She motioned toward the gray sleuth.

"Did you see Lame Greta?"

DeKok rubbed his chin.

81

"Yes," he answered resignedly, "we were there . . ."

She nodded. Her face was serious.

"I understand . . .. I bet it was in connection with the drowning of Blonde Tina."

"Exactly."

She shook her head. Her expression was full of pity.

"What a way to end. And so young." Her tone changed. "But if you ask me . . . it was her own fault."

"How's that?"

She folded her arms, pushing out her bosom.

"It could never last. You could see that. That guy lived on top of a volcano."

"Uncle Rickie?"

"Yes . . . that Uncle Rickie. The guy threw his money around. I've seen it. Unbelievable what he could spend in a single night. He behaved like an oil-sheik on holiday. You see . . . that kind of money . . . nobody can earn that honestly."

"What do you mean? You think he stole?"

Limburger Lena rubbed the tip of her nose with the back of her hand and snorted explicitly.

"What else could it be? Of course he stole! Anything that wasn't nailed down. For years. At least as long as I've known him." She counted on her fingers. "That's been at least five years."

DeKok looked at her searchingly.

"Did you ever have him as a customer?"

A tired smile played around her lips.

"Of course I tried. More than once . . . who wouldn't? After all, I don't do this for my health and a big spender like that . . . it's every working girl's dream. But he didn't want me. Uncle Rickie only liked blondes."

"Like Tina."

"That's what he liked," she said resignedly. "For a blonde he would do anything." She paused. "But Tina shouldn't have smothered him like that. You understand? She should have given him more room . . . give the other girls a chance. That way they could make some money, too. But not Tina. It caused a lot of bad blood."

DeKok looked at her evenly.

"Are you trying to tell me that they have been killed by some pimps . . . or some girls?"

She tapped her forehead with a crooked finger.

"Where are your brains, DeKok? Of course not. Maybe . . . just maybe they might have roughed *her* up a little bit . . . because she kept him to herself. But nobody would have touched Uncle Rickie. A john? You don't kill the goose that lays the golden eggs. You just don't. Besides, roughing up customers is bad for business."

"But what if the goose had a lot of eggs on him?"

Lena gave him a thoughtful look.

"Did he?"

DeKok smiled at her and walked away.

Vledder followed close behind.

* * *

When they returned to Warmoes Street, the Watch Commander looked up from his register as they passed by.

"I have a message for you guys. That dark-blue Jaguar has been found. Didn't you send a telex to that effect?"

DeKok nodded and came closer.

"It's been a few days. Where was it found?"

The Watch Commander studied his notes.

"In the old Cologne Canal, close by the paper-mill of Rath and Dethfever."

"Who found it?"

"The skipper of a sand barge. He noticed it when he apparently went aground where he shouldn't have gone aground. He manoeuvred around the obstacle and notified the bridge keeper near Duivendrecht. He alerted the State Police. When they discovered it was the Jaguar you were interested in, they notified our own Technical Department."

"And?"

The Watch Commander again studied his notes, as if reluctant to share the information. He pursed his lips and then continued.

"Nothing special. Technically the car was in perfect operating order."

"Was it empty?"

The man behind the counter smiled.

"There was nobody in the car . . . if that's what you mean. Other than that it was the usual collection of stuff one gathers in a car. The guys from Technical assume it was driven into the water from the Weesp side."

"On purpose?"

The Watch Commander nodded.

"Absolutely. The car was in first gear."

* * *

DeKok nursed his tired feet. He pulled them up with difficulty and rubbed his painful calves. Then he leaned back in his chair and with a sigh of relief he placed his legs on top of the desk. Slowly the pain dissipated and made room for some cool, calm reflection.

The latest developments in the investigation had surprised him slightly. Lame Greta's information that Richard Vankerk had filled a responsible position within the Community of

Brothers and Sisters, gave a new direction to the search. It certainly was an indication that the murders had *something* to do with the Brothers and Sisters of the Holy Blessings.

During his long career DeKok had encountered a number of religious sects. In a country that had more than three hundred recognized, "official" religions, the number of sects, or quasi sects must be at least double. He knew the type of difficulties he was likely to encounter. It was not easy to penetrate behind the veil of these secret societies. But he had no choice. He was convinced of one thing: Somewhere within the inner circle of the Community was the solution. There the threads of all the loose ends would come together.

He lifted his legs from the desk and commenced to pace up and down the large detective room. His thoughts went over every detail he had so far uncovered. Slowly he let them pass in review.

He started with the proper Mr. and Mrs. Shoebeek. Just returned from a vacation at Cortina d'Ampezzo, they request a special meeting of the members of the society. They have, they stated in their request, undergone a shocking experience. But before the meeting can be called, both are fished lifeless from the waters of Emperors Canal.

What was this "shocking experience" . . . had they heard something? Seen something? Why did they have to die? So strange . . . with entwined fingers, linked arms . . . Why?

And the second couple. Blonde Tina and Richard Vankerk . . . an ambitious little whore and a man who had obviously a lot of money to spend. What was the sense in their death? Was there a clue in the nine-minute telephone conversation with Cortina d'Ampezzo?

DeKok raked his hands through his hair. The pain in his feet came back. The solution, he realized, was a long way off.

He stopped in front of Vledder's desk.

"No news from Italy?"

Young Vledder shook his head and smiled.

"That may be a while. The Italian police is in no hurry and you can't expect much from Interpol. Perhaps we should have called the hotel ourselves."

The gray sleuth grimaced.

"Albergo Cristallo a la Viale Bernini," he pronounced with strange sounds and an atrocious accent. "As you can tell, my Italian is virtually non-existent. We could try with an interpreter. But it remains problematical if the management of a hotel will release any information about their guests over the telephone." He looked pensive. "I don't think so. No," he decided, "we have no choice . . . we have to await the results of the activities of our Italian colleagues."

He fell silent, pulled his lower lip and let it plop back. Finally he looked again at Vledder and spoke:

"Richard Vankerk's car . . . what about the report on the blue Jaguar?"

Vledder shrugged his shoulders.

"They just wanted to get rid of it."

DeKok shook his head.

"I mean *where* it was found."

"In the Cologne Canal, near Rath and Dethfever?"

DeKok nodded.

"Doesn't that ring a bell?"

Vledder stared at him. For a few seconds his face remained expressionless. Then it cleared up.

"Duivendrecht," he exclaimed suddenly, "the temple of the Community."

8

They proceeded at a snail's pace through the narrow streets, along the canals through the busy traffic of the inner city. Vledder drove the car with easy competence and DeKok was slouched down in his seat. That way he could observe the rooftops with fond attention and did not have to look at the traffic. DeKok despised cars and all things mechanical. He freely admitted to being the worst driver in Holland, perhaps all of Europe. After a while he finally tore his gaze away from the picturesque gables and, pushing his hat further back on his head, looked at Vledder.

"You have all the necessary information?"

The young Inspector nodded slowly, not taking his eyes off the road.

"It took a bit of doing. It wasn't easy. But finally I *did* locate someone who was willing to talk."

"Somebody connected to the Community?"

Vledder nodded.

"A simple Brother who became really enthusiastic when I hinted that I was interested in becoming a member."

"You didn't!"

"I'm sorry," smiled Vledder, "but I'm afraid I did. I certainly led him to believe that I wanted to become a member.

He told me that the Community of the Brothers and Sisters of the Holy Blessings had been in existence for more than forty years. The founder was a Hubert Hoekstra, better known as Hubert, son of Johannes by Wilhelmina, a devout fisherman from Enkhuizen who was of the opinion that the Reformed Church, of which he was a member, did not take enough notice of the Holy Blessings."

"So . . . he went in business for himself."

Vledder looked serious.

"Yes, but not the way you mean. It's almost certain that he founded the Community from the purest of motives, because of a profound belief. From the many stories about him, it's certain that he was an honest and sober man who gathered quite a following in a relatively short time because of his devout piety. Not until after his death did the leaders introduce additional, strange rituals and urge the Brothers and Sisters to make substantial sacrifices."

"The Community is rich, I take it?"

Vledder nodded emphatically.

"You can say that again . . . although nobody is certain about the total extent of their possessions. It is certain that the current leader of the Community, Brother Rigobertus, lives in a mortgage-free capital villa near Hilversum . . . not exactly a cheap part of Holland. He is also known to have at least two so-called vacation homes . . . there may be others."

DeKok pushed himself in a more upright position.

"Has the temple of the Community always been in Duivendrecht?"

Vledder shook his head.

"That's something more recent. Ever since the paper-mill has been abandoned. In the early days they gathered in an old house in Amsterdam."

DeKok gave him a sharp look.

"At Emperors Canal?"

Vledder nodded, pursing his lips.

"I went to take a look. It's barely fifty meters from the place where the corpses were found in the water."

DeKok pushed his lower lip forward and snorted.

"Does the Community still own the house?"

"Yep," answered Vledder, doing something incomprehensible to the gearbox of the dilapidated VW, causing the car to suddenly jump forward, after which it settled down with an offended growl. DeKok ignored the antics of the car.

"Go on," he urged his young friend.

"Well, I checked it out. It is currently being used as an office, at least part of the premises is. Then there are some rooms for discussion groups. Discussions about religious experiences, meetings with the Devil and that sort of thing. But the important meetings are reserved for the temple in Duivendrecht. The baptismal services, too, are exclusively reserved for the temple."

"Baptismal services?"

Vledder nodded slowly.

"Yes, in the past, before the temple was founded, they used to take place in the public swimming pool. They used to rent it for a specific time. But no longer . . . there's a shallow pool in the temple which is specifically used for the rituals. For each baptismal service the pool is filled with fresh water and the new Brothers and Sisters are completely submerged by the celebrant. It's supposed to be an impressive service."

For a while they drove on in silence. DeKok was absorbing the new information and matching it to the information he already had. Vledder concentrated on driving.

"Scandals?" asked DeKok suddenly. "Rumors?"

Vledder looked pensive.

"The Brother who was giving me information was rather guarded on that point. He obviously was trying to protect the reputation of the Community. But lately there are whispers among the Brothers and Sisters about certain . . . eh, excesses."

DeKok was surprised.

"What sort of excesses?"

Vledder made a sad gesture with one hand, before he switched on the turn signal.

"My informant would not talk about it. Of course I tried to pin him down, but to no avail. Then, when he found out I was a cop, he clammed up altogether. The only thing he agreed to do was to set up this appointment."

"With the illustrious Brother Rigobertus."

Vledder nodded with an expressionless face.

"He has granted us an audience."

* * *

The gray brick wall with glass shards cemented in the top looked unassailable and hostile. It was a high wall and seemed to lean outward as an extra discouragement to would-be climbers.

Inspector DeKok looked up at the top of the wall. It must be at least ten feet high, he estimated. Carefully, searching they paced its length. The heavy wall seemed to enclose the entire area. The bastion had no weak spots.

After a thorough reconnoitre they stepped back for several feet and tried to look at the entire structure. They remained silent and impressed until Vledder finally broke the silence. He shook his head in amazement.

"This is supposed to be a temple? It looks more like a maximum-security prison, or a nut-house from a less enlightened era."

DeKok nodded agreement.

"Religion also thinks in centuries," he remarked cryptically.

90

A wide gravel path, flanked by severely trimmed conifers, led to a large, heavy gate of intricate cast-iron. Behind the gate was the dark tunnel of the gate-house. As they approached, the gate slid silently aside and disappeared in the wall.

There was nobody in sight. Carefully they entered and the heavy gate slammed shut behind them.

From a side door, formed by a gothic arch, a man approached. He was small and wore a gray duster, the unofficial uniform of janitors and concierges all over Europe. He folded his hands in front of his chest and bowed in a manner reminiscent of Hindu greetings.

"My name is Brother Cornelis," he said in a soft, almost whispering tone of voice. "Your arrival has been announced. You are both awaited. Allow me to precede you."

He turned around and walked away from them.

The door through which he had appeared, led to a spacious lobby. Imperceptibly the lobby gave way to an even larger space. Large glass-in-lead windows provided a diffused, yellowish light. The entire floor was covered with a soft, cream-colored Berber carpet upon which, approximately in the center, were stacked hundreds of small, wine-colored, velvet pillows.

DeKok looked around carefully, absorbing every detail. He was looking for the shallow pool, the baptismal font, but was unable to discover it.

At the end of the large room, Brother Cornelis sidled in between some purple curtains and knocked respectfully on a heavy oak door beyond. He waited a few seconds and then slowly pressed down on the heavy brass door handle. The door opened soundlessly.

Behind a large, circular desk stood a short, compact man. Long, dark hair, interspersed with gray hung down to his shoulders. DeKok estimated him to be in his early fifties. He was dressed in a wide, formless, toga-like garment of home-spun fabric, bordered with a large, black edge.

"Brother Rigobertus," he announced himself cheerfully in a deep base voice.

He made a slight bow in the direction of the two Inspectors and produced a ham-like hand from somewhere inside the toga.

DeKok approached. Slowly, thoughtfully. Meanwhile his sharp gaze studied the face in front of him; the pug nose, the pink, somewhat fleshy cheeks, the wide mouth with the full lips. DeKok was convinced that Brother Rigobertus did *not* live an ascetic life. With a reserved smile he pressed the outstretched hand. Despite its size, the Brother's hand felt clammy and weak.

"DeKok," announced the sleuth simply. ". . . with kay-oh-kay. Detective-Inspector DeKok, attached to Warmoes Street station." He turned slightly away. "And this is Detective-Inspector Vledder . . . my valuable assistant."

"With whom you are blessed," spoke Brother Rigobertus solemnly.

DeKok nodded, slightly taken aback.

"Blessed," he stammered. "Yes, yes, indeed . . . blessed."

Brother Rigobertus emerged from behind the enormous desk and gestured toward some easy chairs in a corner of the large room.

"Shall we seat ourselves there?" He produced what was meant to be a charming smile. "I take it that your visit is of a professional nature?"

The gray sleuth inclined his head and looked sad.

"We came to pay our respects, to offer our condolences, concerning the recent loss of the Shoebeeks and that of Richard Vankerk. They were . . . eh, according to my information, all three members of your . . . of your Community."

Brother Rigobertus nodded unhappily.

"It was a deep, sad shock to us all," he said somberly. "First Brother Castor and his wife and shortly thereafter Brother Christian. And him in company with . . . with, eh, a woman of questionable morals." He looked at DeKok. "Let me assure you that both were very much appreciated and are sorely missed."

DeKok's face remained expressionless.

"Was Mr. Shoebeek called Brother Castor?"

Brother Rigobertus made a defensive gesture, as if trying to cast aside the aspersion.

"No, no . . . not called. You make it sound like a nickname." He hesitated momentarily. "He was Brother Castor in our Community, the Community of the Holy Blessings." Again he hesitated. "Or, rather," he continued, "no longer, actually. At the urging of his wife he had long since resigned from the Carillon."

DeKok leaned forward.

"Forgive me," he said in a friendly tone of voice, "we're not familiar with the secrets of your . . . Community. What do you mean by the Carillon?"

Brother Rigobertus brought his hands together and allowed the fingertips to rest against each other. There was a superior, almost supercilious smile on his lips.

"As leader of the Community, I am supported and advised by the Carillon. That is our name for it. It is a clear-sounding name and we bestow it upon the four highest functionaries of the Community. The name must always start with a 'C'."

"Like Castor?"

The spiritual leader nodded agreeably as if DeKok had just answered a very difficult question with a clever answer.

"But as I said," he went on, "Brother Castor resigned from the Carillon about a month ago. Needless to say, he remained a member in good standing of the Community. But his function in the Carillon was taken over by Brother Crispin."

DeKok glanced at Vledder.

"We've met Brother Crispin."

Brother Rigobertus rubbed a rosy cheek.

"An excellent choice, I *must* say. Brother Crispin is a very dedicated young man, a great support for me. Devout, loyal, committed to the cause."

DeKok coughed emphatically.

"Richard Vankerk was also a member of the Carillon?"

Brother Rigobertus reacted sharply and a bit surprised.

"Certainly, to be sure. As Brother Christian he had a great deal of influence."

"In what way?"

The spiritual leader made a grand gesture.

"Brother Christian was our treasurer. He was in charge of our finances, he determined the goals and objectives of our various charitable works." He leaned back in his chair with a dramatic sigh. "It will be very difficult to find a suitable successor."

DeKok ignored the remark and the by-play.

"Who are the other members of the Carillon?"

Brother Rigobertus raised a hand in the air.

"There is Brother Constantin, the, I would almost say fanatical, but above all enthusiastic son out of Brother Christian's first matrimonial alliance and Brother Cornelis, our audiophile. He received you at the gate, earlier." He remained silent for a while. "A friendly and above all, devout man. He was already a member of the Carillon before I assumed the burden of leadership. He is a man without any pretensions. He's too shy, too self-effacing. He always wears that gray duster. Many people, upon first acquaintance, think he's the janitor."

DeKok gave the burdened leader a questioning look.

"Audiophile? I'm not familiar with that word."

Brother Rigobertus smiled indulgently.

"Brother Cornelis is besotted with sound. It's marvelous what he can do with it. He records all our songs and prayers. Because of him, even the dead will sing in our gatherings." He raised an index finger in the air. "And I can assure you that the blessed voices of Brother Christian and Brother Castor and his wife will not be lost. They will sing around our tabernacle from now until eternity."

The gray sleuth closed his eyes. It was a tired gesture. The oily, self-satisfied voice of Brother Rigobertus irritated him to no end. For a moment he wished himself on a lake somewhere, or along a river, with no other worry than whether or not the fish would bite.

The moment did not last long. He shrugged himself back into the present.

"They are dead," he remarked sharply. "And what's more, they have been murdered."

The spiritual leader looked shocked. His pink, fleshy cheeks quivered. Nervously his tongue darted out and licked his lips.

"Murdered?" he asked hoarsely.

DeKok merely nodded.

"You were absolutely correct," he said evenly. "Our visit is indeed of a professional nature." He gave the other a long, hard stare. "We're looking for the killer among your flock."

Brother Rigobertus came abruptly to his feet. His hands balled into fists and there was a strange light in his eyes.

"That's insane," he cried excitedly. "We're a community of happy people, who rejoice in God's word and who are open to receiving His Blessings." He shook his head. "It's absurd to assume that we, that god-fearing people . . ."

DeKok waved his arms with a rejecting motion.

"A great many murders have been committed in the name of religion," he interrupted. "Religious beliefs are no guarantee of innocence."

Brother Rigobertus sighed as if a balloon had been punctured. Slowly he fell back in his chair.

"But who could possibly be interested in the death of those people." His tone had become calm, convincing. "Brother Castor and his wife were good people."

DeKok grimaced.

"But I understand that Brother Christian was *not* so good. If I'm informed correctly, it's not unlikely that on occasion he has been known to use the funds of the believers to . . . eh, entertain himself, shall we say?"

Brother Rigobertus shrugged his shoulders. The revelation did not seem to shock him in the least.

"Everybody in our Community has his own task," he said resignedly. "We do not check on our treasurer. Trust begets trust."

DeKok smiled and shook his head.

"That's hardly realistic. The fact is that trust more often than not is repaid with betrayal. Legally it's called betrayal of a fiduciary position." He paused. "I don't think it's entirely outside the realm of expectations that a few Brothers and Sisters knew about Brother Christian's excesses . . . and regretted them."

"But surely *that* doesn't justify murder!"

DeKok gave the spiritual leader a sharp look.

"Does that exist? Justification for murder?"

Brother Rigobertus did not answer at once. Clearly he pondered his response. After a while he looked up.

"I'm afraid that murder, no matter how, is never justifiable." His voice was soft, barely above a whisper. "And that is why, Inspector, if you persist in thinking that the murderer is to be found in our Community, I give you leave to take whatever steps you think necessary in respect to the Brothers and Sisters." He paused, folded his hands on his chest. "But I do hope that I may count on a certain amount of discretion on your part? You know as well as I how easy it is for a group such as ours to become the focus of a scandal."

DeKok rose slowly.

"You may rest assured that we'll be discreet," he said calmly. Suddenly he leaned both hands on the desk and brought his face close to that of Brother Rigobertus, who had remained seated. "Have *women* ever been members of the Carillon?"

The question obviously touched upon a sore point. Brother Rigobertus looked up, a watchful glance in his eyes.

"Just once," he replied shortly. "Sister Charisse. She had been recommended because of her innocence."

"And?"

For a moment the Brother pressed his lips together. Then he spoke tonelessly:

"She hanged herself."

9

Brother Cornelis led the way. Brother Rigobertus had asked him to show the two Inspectors to the door. DeKok increased his speed slightly and came to walk alongside their guide.

"Brother Rigobertus spoke very highly of you," he opened the conversation with a smile.

Brother Cornelis glanced aside.

"He did . . . did he?"

DeKok nodded emphatically.

"Especially your remarkable gifts concerning audio equipment was highly appreciated. He said that you were able to make the dead sing."

A soft smile fled across the pale face.

"We've always been blessed with good voices," he said enthusiastically. "Especially 1976 was a good year for voices. I make every new Brother and Sister sing our songs and prayers. I store those voices. When they have passed on, I mix the dead voices with the living choirs. That's how the dead sing with the living. It's very stimulating. It reinforces the thoughts of eternity." He gave the old sleuth a searching look. "Are you interested?"

DeKok nodded.

"Yes, I am," he said.

Brother Cornelis glanced up and stretched out an arm toward the dark ceiling.

"Up there," he explained, "there are more than a hundred loudspeakers, in various sizes. I have made most of them myself." He smiled. "The ready-made boxes don't always have the sound I'm looking for." Again he pointed up. "Low notes are not as critical. I mean, it's not too important how they are reproduced. Therefore they are more off to the side. But the middle registers and the high notes generally determine the overall quality of the sound. That's why I have a large concentration of tweeters right in the center . . . those are smaller speakers for higher notes," he added. "In addition, I've installed a number of sound panels so the sound can be directed indirectly as well and give it more color."

He walked toward a side door, opened it and showed a room full of electronic equipment. With experienced hands he adjusted dials and closed contacts. He walked back and took the Inspectors by the arm.

"Go stand in the center, in the spot normally occupied by the choir. The sound is perfect, no matter where, but that's the spot at which it's aimed . . . to support the living choir, you understand."

Suddenly the sound came closer. It seemed to approach from all sides simultaneously . . . mighty and irresistible. A powerful choir gained in strength as DeKok walked toward the indicated spot. "Nearer my God to thee," descended on him and smothered him like a blanket of heavenly sound.

DeKok closed his eyes to shut out his surroundings. He felt as if he were carried away on melodious waves of music, became a part of the choir and suddenly he felt an irresistible urge to sing along. He opened his mouth and his raucous base voice mixed with the other voices. Somehow it was not a disturbing influence, but a necessary underlining of the perfect voices around him.

Brother Cornelis beamed.

"Nice . . . isn't it? It took me a lot of years to get it to this point. Sound is a strange media. You know what it is, how it is created. You can record it, play it back. There are big industries that specialize in sound, who manufacture the equipment. But only a few know anything about the color of sound . . . how to give it warmth . . . how to make it a *living* experience. They're too wrapped up in making it technically perfect . . . HiFi, CDs . . . all means nothing unless you can *feel* the living artists."

He gestured around.

"An old factory . . . from the 18th Century. Built as a sweat shop. What sort of acoustics are to be expected? For years I listened in every spot of the great hall, experimented, adjusted . . . until I discovered all the dissonants."

The gray sleuth did not react to the words. He stared at nothing in particular and listened intently to the last notes of "Nearer my God." When the sound finally died away, he sighed deeply and nodded.

"Dissonants," he said somberly, "dissonants are everywhere." He paused. "Even among the Brothers and Sisters of the Holy Blessings."

Brother Cornelis looked at him intently, a deep crease in his forehead. He gestured toward DeKok.

"But even dissonants have a purpose," he said earnestly. "How would we be able to appreciate pure tones if we did not have dissonants as comparison? It is the same with good people and bad people. Because so many are filled with bad thoughts, it's a relief to find an honest and good person."

DeKok smiled.

"You are a wise man," he praised. "As wise as Brother Rigobertus."

The Brother's face became hard and expressionless. His green eyes flickered a warning.

"Brother Rigobertus," he hissed, "is the snake in Paradise."

DeKok looked at him, feigning ignorance.

"Snake?" he repeated.

Brother Cornelis nodded slowly.

"A forked tongue . . . and in service of the Devil."

* * *

They drove away from the old factory and headed back toward Amsterdam. It was drizzling and the wipers made their hypnotic sweep across the windshield. DeKok reached over and shut down the communication gear. He rummaged in his pockets and came up with a dusty piece of hard candy. Carelessly he brushed off the dust and put the sweet in his mouth. He sucked contently for a while. Then he looked as his young partner.

"You're awfully quiet. I hardly heard a sound from you all afternoon. Didn't you have any questions?"

Vledder shrugged.

"I think we're barking up the wrong tree."

"How's that?"

Vledder made an impatient gesture with his hand before he dropped it back on the gearshift.

"The Community of the Brothers and Sisters of the Holy Blessings looks too peaceful to me. The beautiful temple, that heavenly music . . . I find it hard to connect it all with crime, violence, murder." He fell silent, a serious look on his face. "When I stood outside that impregnable wall," he continued, "I could still believe it."

"Crime, violence, murder?"

Vledder nodded.

"Yes, then. It had reality . . . something concrete."

DeKok pushed his hat farther back on his head.

102

"But now that you've been inside you feel different?" There was puzzlement in his voice.

Vledder sighed.

"I don't know," he said, irritated. "Murder requires a motive. And to find that motive among them . . . it troubles me."

DeKok hoisted himself up in the narrow seat.

"In that case . . . where would you like to look? We have to keep in mind that the late Mr. Shoebeek was also a member of the Carillon . . . months ago. And that certainly seems to point toward the Brothers and Sisters."

Vledder pressed his lips together and shook his head.

"I don't agree," he said finally. "You're wrong, somehow. You're not thinking straight."

DeKok was amazed.

"Not thinking straight," he asked skeptically.

The young Inspector nodded decisively.

"Your reasoning goes as follows: the victims, Shoebeek and Vankerk, in their guises as Brother Castor and Brother Christian belonged to the Community . . . to the Carillon . . . therefore the perpetrator must also belong to the Community of the Holy Blessings." He rubbed the tip of his nose in an unconscious imitation of one of DeKok's mannerisms. "A simplistic way of thinking," he added, grinning.

"Perhaps."

Vledder gave his mentor a challenging look.

"Is it not much more likely that the perpetrator is *outside* the Community," he demanded.

DeKok acted obtuse.

"Why?"

It was too much for Vledder. Usually such a careful driver, he lifted both hands from the steering wheel and gestured wildly. The old VW started to veer almost immediately and he hastily brought the car back under control.

"Just consider hate, envy, animosity. There are so many of these religious sects that fight each other bitterly, where the members of one group just as soon drink the blood of another. The fact that two of the higher functionaries of the Community have fallen victim, gives *me* food for thought."

DeKok did not answer. He tried to follow the train of thought of his young friend. When he was unable to do so, he pressed his hat further down over his eyes and sank resignedly down in the seat.

Vledder continued enthusiastically.

"Just think, for a moment, about the death of Richard Vankerk with Blonde Tina, a whore from the District. For an opposing sect that is a god-given opportunity to prove how godless and how, how . . . *wrong* the Community is." He smiled at DeKok. "What exactly was the way Brother Constantin put it?"

The gray sleuth growled from below his hat.

"The Evil One has done his work," he quoted. "Chained to the object of his sins . . . he descends into the bottomless pit."

Vledder laughed out loud.

"Amen!" he roared.

* * *

DeKok knocked softly on the closed door. When he heard a distinct "Yes," from the other side, he pushed against the door and stepped inside. Commissaris Buitendam gave him a prim smile and pushed aside a number of reports. The Commissaris pointed at a chair in front of his desk.

"Sit down, DeKok," he said in a friendly tone of voice. "I take it that you've come to tell me how you have returned from the errors of your ways."

DeKok seated himself carefully.

"I don't understand . . . eh, what you mean."

The Commissaris gestured expansively.

"That crazy idea of yours," he rebuked gently, "that those people, those from the canal . . ." He looked up, irked. "What canal was that again?"

"Emperors Canal."

"Exactly, yes . . . Emperors Canal . . . that those people died because of a crime."

"Murdered."

"Yes, yes . . . murdered."

DeKok shook his head slowly. He tapped his fingers on the right side of his chest.

"I . . . I don't have to return from the error of my ways," he said with a grin. "I have not strayed."

The commissarial face fell.

"Do you have any indications of foul play?" he asked with suspicion in his voice.

DeKok rubbed his chin.

"No . . . clear indications . . . no, I do not have any *clear* indications."

The commissarial face relaxed. The eyes suddenly sparkled.

"You do not," he repeated slowly. It sounded relieved. He immediately resumed his usual, regal pose. "Then I will so inform the Judge-Advocate. I will advise him to close the file." He smiled at DeKok. "It will be a load off his mind, I'm sure. You see, DeKok," he continued confidentially, "you have a certain reputation as a sleuth. Everyone is well aware of your qualifications. It remains a risky business to disagree with that much experience."

DeKok nodded calmly.

"That is why I once more urge a complete autopsy."

The Commissaris looked at him, red dots of anger appeared on his cheeks.

"You know the opinion of the Judge-Advocate in the matter," he said heatedly.

DeKok clapped his hands together.

"But that view, in my opinion, shows the error of *his* ways. If we do not do an autopsy . . . and preferably as soon as possible, we will lose important clues. Now it's still possible. I can still lay my hands on the corpses and Dr. Rusteloos has agreed to work through the night, if necessary." He made a compelling gesture toward the phone. "Call the Judge-Advocate and try to persuade him."

"Do you have new evidence?"

"No . . . nothing substantial."

"Then I won't call."

With a deep sigh, DeKok leaned forward.

"Tomorrow will be too late," he said pleadingly. "At ten o'clock all the victims will be cremated. Now you can still stop it."

"No."

DeKok rose. He pointed an accusing finger at his Chief.

"Ignorance can be an excuse for stupidity," he said, "but obstinacy is no excuse, ever." He paused and then changed his tone of voice. "When the case is solved, I'll remind you of this interview."

"Is that a threat?" asked the Commissaris dangerously.

The gray detective looked at him and shook his head.

"No threats . . . just a friendly promise to discuss mismanagement."

Commissaris Buitendam swallowed. His Adam's apple bobbed up and down and he clearly had trouble articulating.

"OUT!" he roared finally.

DeKok left.

* * *

When he returned to the detective room, Vledder gave him a searching look.

"You saw the Commissaris?"

"I tried to persuade him to order an autopsy," answered DeKok.

"Success?"

DeKok shook his head sadly.

"I was sent from the room again, for a change. He would not listen. Without clear and I repeat *clear* indications of a crime he did not feel he could bother the Judge-Advocate. I contemplated going over his head . . . but he was already upset enough." He stopped in front of the desk. "In the case of a regular funeral we would still have a chance. If we discover something definitive, we could always, as a last resort, get an order for exhumation."

"Exhumation?"

"Yes, unbury them so to speak."

"I know what exhumation means," answered Vledder, a bit stiffly. "But why?"

"To check the corpses for the presence of poison."

"Poison?"

"Yes a poison that renders the victim helpless."

Vledder looked at him and swallowed.

"But they drowned . . ."

The gray sleuth nodded thoughtfully.

"Yes . . . drowning is the immediate, the apparent cause of death. That's official. But as I have pointed out before . . . murder by drowning is not easy. On the contrary. That's why I don't believe it. Especially not in these cases. I have a strong suspicion that the victims were first rendered helpless . . . doped, for instance."

The young Inspector stared at his older colleague.

"And then drowned?"

"Very good," answered DeKok, pointing at Vledder. "Perhaps they were thrown in the canal while they were unconscious. They still breathe, but are unable to help themselves. Ergo, they drown and that also explains the water in the lungs." He paused and sighed. "Now you know why I'm so insistent on an autopsy. After a cremation we can only sift through the ashes . . . virtually impossible to detect any poisons."

Vledder looked pensive.

"Is there no way to prevent the cremation?"

DeKok shook his head.

"Impossible. we don't have a legal leg to stand on."

"Now what?"

DeKok stared into the distance. Without realizing it he moved toward the window and looked out over the rooftops of the ancient District. His domain . . . the old inner city of Amsterdam, including the Red Light District and part of the *Jordaan*. Jordaan, reflected DeKok, a Dutch bastardization of the French word *jardin*, meaning garden. Nobody remembered why the French Huguenots who settled there after escaping the persecution in France called that part of town a garden. There was little left that would remind one of a garden. Except that all the streets were, and still are, named after flowers.

With an effort he brought his mind back to the present.

"But despite all obstacles . . . I will get to the bottom of this affair . . . I *will* solve it." He turned around and pointed at Vledder. "Tomorrow you go to the Municipal Crematorium West Garden, it's on Oaklake Road. You will make a note of those who are interested in the ceremony." He paused and rubbed the bridge of his nose with a little finger. "And try to find out," he added, "why our victims did not select a normal, Christian burial."

"What do you mean by 'Christian' burial?"

DeKok shook his head, smiling.

"Religious persons usually do not opt for cremation. That's supposed to be in contradiction with God's final judgement . . . the concept of Resurrection. In early days," he digressed, "it used to be part of the Law that everyone had a right to a *Christian* burial. That meant whole, all parts intact, to be buried in a church, or in a church yard . . . and for Roman-Catholics . . . in hallowed ground."

The young Inspector frowned.

"And you want to know why the religious Brothers and Sisters of the Holy Blessings choose other than a 'Christian' burial?"

DeKok nodded approval.

"Got it in one. Perhaps there was somebody who thought that cremation was safer . . . for him, or her."

Vledder rubbed his hands together and looked cheerful.

"You know, I'm starting to get interested again."

The Watch Commander, Kamphouse, entered the room and threaded his way to DeKok's desk. He placed a long, yellow envelope in DeKok's hands.

"From Interpol," explained Kamphouse.

"Thanks," said DeKok, "I appreciate you bringing it up yourself."

Kamphouse grunted and left. DeKok opened the envelope.

"Finally some information from our Italian colleagues," he said as he unfolded the letter and started to read. Then he looked up and gave Vledder a look of utter bewilderment.

"Do you know who was in Cortina d'Ampezzo on that fateful day?"

"No, who?"

DeKok swallowed, looked at the letter as if wanting to verify what he had just read.

"Monique Vankerk. She shared an apartment with a certain Marius Heeteren."

Vledder's mouth fell open.

"Marius Heeteren," he gasped, "that's the worldly name of Brother Rigobertus."

10

It was busy on the Damrak, but that was no surprise. The street is the main artery between the Central Station and what most people consider to be the heart of Amsterdam: Dam Square. A tentative, mild and shy spring sun had chased away the Dutch rain and dampness and had succeeded in enticing Amsterdammers and foreigners alike into spring walks. The flags waved gaily on the piers for the tour boats and an early barrel organ mixed its unique sound with the babble of voices. The smell of raw herring, the first of the season, overpowered most other aromas. Spring was just around the corner and it vibrated in the air.

DeKok pushed back his hat and opened his overcoat. He glanced at Vledder.

"What about the cremation?" he asked.

"What about it?'

"You went?"

"This morning," admitted Vledder.

"Well?"

Vledder seemed reluctant to tear himself away from the light-hearted atmosphere all around them. Finally he shrugged, as if reconciled to his fate.

"A pitiful spectacle," said the young man. "I could have stayed home."

"Why?"

"There was almost nobody there."

"Nobody?" DeKok looked at his colleague. "There were no Brothers and Sisters of the Holy Blessing?"

Vledder shook his head sadly.

"It was really noticeable. The entire Community shined by its absence. Not even the big man, Leader Brother Rigobertus showed up. Not a single member of the Carillon. Monique Vankerk and Rosita Stuyvenberg were also absent. Lame Greta was there . . . and the Shoebeek son. I spoke with both of them."

"Any results?"

"I especially wanted to know why Mr. Shoebeek had left the Carillon. But the son didn't have a clue. He did add that his mother had been against it from the beginning. His mother, according to the son, had not hesitated to make her opinion known about that. Apparently she had a particular dislike for Brother Christian. She didn't trust him."

"Richard Vankerk?"

"Exactly. 'That guy is a thief,' she used to say, 'He wines and dines and tries to get every woman he meets.' "

"Bold talk."

Vledder nodded.

"Mother Shoebeek must have been a formidable woman. The son assumes that the request for a special meeting of the Community must have been her idea."

DeKok pushed his lower lip forward while he stared at a herring stand. His eyes narrowed in contemplation.

"But you found out nothing about the reason for the request?" he asked finally.

"No," said Vledder.

"And what about Lame Greta?"

112

The younger man smiled tenderly.

"She was very nice. She seemed to be the only one present who genuinely cared . . . was really sad. When I started talking about Blonde Tina, she started to cry. I asked why Rickie and Tina were not buried at Sorrow Field, as she had said."

"And?"

Vledder shrugged, trying to distract DeKok's attention from the herring stand.

"It was somebody from the Community. He visited her and convinced her to agree to a cremation."

"Who?"

"Brother Crispin."

"Well, well," said DeKok softly. Then the lure of the herring became too much for him. He pulled Vledder with him and approached the stand. Before long he had a raw herring filet by the tail, dragged it through the raw, chopped onions and with two, three bites, his head bent far backward, he ate the delicacy. Vledder had just finished his first herring, when DeKok threw the tail of his second herring in the receptacle. He looked at Vledder who shook his head. DeKok hesitated, looking at the platter of herrings waiting to be enjoyed. Then he manfully controlled himself from having another one and paid for the three herrings.

* * *

"Is this it?"

Vledder nodded.

"128 Brewers Canal. This is where Monique and Richard Vankerk used to live."

"You think she's home?"

Vledder shrugged his shoulders.

"I would have told her we'd be coming to see her, if I had seen her at the cremation, this morning."

DeKok smiled.

"Maybe it's better this way. An unexpected visit can have advantages ... sometimes."

He pulled on the intricately worked, brass bell-pull. Somewhere deep in the bowels of the house they heard the sound of a bell. The gray sleuth rubbed the bridge of his nose with a little finger and grinned.

"I wonder if she wears black."

"Why?"

DeKok grinned again.

"It's expected, you know. Black is the traditional dress for a sorrowing widow." He glanced up at the facade of the house. "Did they live alone, or are there other people living in the house?"

Vledder shook his head. He knew what DeKok meant. These large houses in the city, especially those along the more prestigious canals, had long since become too expensive for the average citizen. Those that had not been converted to offices, were usually chopped up into small flats, condominiums, or rooming houses.

"I don't think so," said Vledder. "The house is, or was, sole property of Richard Vankerk. Not even a mortgage. At the time of his death, Monique was still the legal spouse. I don't know if the two sons, from the marriage to Rosita Stuyvenberg, can make a claim. I don't think the will has been read yet and if it has, suits have not yet been filed." He grimaced. "I know from bitter experience with my own family. Those inheritance cases can take forever."

"Did he have any other property?"

"Hard to tell. Richard Vankerk was a wheeler-dealer. He did more or less what he wanted and kept no records, other than in his head. There's not even a clear differentiation between his private property and the assets of the Community."

DeKok snorted.

"That's going to be a proper mess. Especially for us. It will be difficult to determine who would benefit from his death."

"You got that right," agreed Vledder.

"And where," asked DeKok, "did you get *that* expression?"

Vledder grinned sheepishly.

"Movies," he mumbled.

Before DeKok could lecture him on the detrimental influences of movie language on conversational etiquette, the heavy front door opened slowly. Monique's gold-blonde hair shone in the half darkness of the corridor behind her. Her hair swirled in luxurious waves around her shoulders. She wore a tight, unrelieved black dress with long sleeves and a high collar.

For just a moment DeKok caught his breath. Her appearance caused the same numbing, bewitching experience as during their first meeting. The exquisite contours of her figure and the warm glow of her personality whispered sweet promises of intimate delights. She smiled sweetly.

"I was expecting you."

DeKok swallowed.

"We . . . eh, we had meant to surprise you," he stammered shyly.

She did not react but made an inviting gesture and led both men into the house.

From the foyer they entered a long, wide marble corridor. At the end she opened a door which led to a large room, decorated with exuberant landscapes on the walls and frivolous plaster cherubims in the corners of the sculpted ceiling. From the center depended the enormous cloud of a sparkling crystal chandelier.

Monique Vankerk pointed at a set of easy chairs of dark oak, covered with yellow and brown brocade.

"Please have a seat," she said in a friendly tone of voice.

The gray sleuth stopped and made it a point to look carefully around the room. Only then did he seat himself across from her. There was a look of amazement in his eyes.

"He's not here?"

She looked confused.

"Who?"

"Brother Rigobertus."

The friendly look disappeared from her face.

"That's an obscene remark."

DeKok nodded resignedly.

"Murder is an obscene business."

A deep frown marred her perfect face.

"You mean that Richard has really been murdered?"

DeKok cocked his head at her.

"How did you think he died?"

She closed her eyes and sighed.

"The Brothers and Sisters of the Holy Blessings believe that Richard committed suicide. That's why he and the Shoebeek couple received an unChristian burial. We're not allowed to kill ourselves. Life is a gift from God. We do not have the right to refuse that privilege. We have to wait until he calls for us."

"You're a member of the community?"

Monique Vankerk nodded.

"You became a member through your marriage to Richard?"

"Yes."

"And you, too, now believe it was suicide?"

She did not answer at once.

"Well . . . I have trouble believing in suicide," she said after some time, hesitation in her voice.

DeKok looked at her with big, surprised eyes.

"But surely," he protested, "that seems inconsistent. What *do* you think? You were the first one to speak of murder."

The young woman lowered her head.

"I know what you mean, but when I came to visit you that day, I came to report a missing person. It had been some time since I had heard from Richard ... I was overwrought ... anxious. When I thought about Richard's turbulent life, I did not think that murder was unthinkable."

"And now?"

She shrugged beautiful shoulders.

"I don't know," she said, unsure of herself. "It's as if I'm groping in the dark. Now, after his death, I have the feeling I never really knew him. I mean, the real Richard, his true character . . . I don't think I ever understood it. All these years . . . I was married to a stranger."

DeKok rubbed the back of his neck. It was a weary gesture.

"But you knew about the relationship with Blonde Tina," he gestured. "That's the woman who was found in the canal with him."

She nodded slowly to herself.

"Richard had many relationships. Sexually he was a glutton."

DeKok's eyes narrowed.

"He ... eh, wanted more than you could give him?"

She raked long, slender fingers through her hair.

"Sexuality," she said softly, "is ... the physical union ... for me it's the apex of love ... not just the act itself."

DeKok nodded his understanding.

"At the time you wanted to make us believe that your marriage to Richard was well nigh perfect."

She reacted sadly.

"A woman likes to pretend . . . that is, I did not want to admit failure."

DeKok leaned closer.

"Did Richard ever mention divorce?"

She looked up at him, suspicion in her eyes.

"Yes, indeed, he did."

"In order to marry Blonde Tina?"

"Yes."

"You agreed to a divorce?"

Monique Vankerk nodded slowly.

"I could not see the use of resisting. Eventually I would lose the battle anyway. That's the way Richard was. Rosita Stuyvenberg couldn't make her marriage last, either. I thought it best to separate as good friends."

DeKok grinned mischievously.

"But you had conditions . . ."

She raised her head proudly, a combative glow in her eyes.

"I wanted him to leave the Community."

"Why?"

"He stole from the faithful."

DeKok laughed, it sounded false, even to his own ears.

"How noble," he mocked.

She made a repentant gesture.

"I just couldn't stand it any longer."

The gray sleuth reacted sharply.

"But he had been stealing from the faithful for years. You *knew* that." His lips clamped down in a disapproving expression. He paused, then he pointed at her. "While you could still benefit from it, make a profit out of it, you kept quiet . . . by your silence you condoned Richard's manipulations, his stealing from the faithful. Only when Richard appeared to be slipping through your fingers . . . when he was about to get away . . . only then did

118

you set as a condition his resignation from the Carillon, from the Community."

She stood up, agitated. She moved her hands above her head in a gesture of bewilderment.

"That isn't true," she said vehemently. "It's simply not true. If I told him once, I told him a thousand times not to swindle the faithful, to embezzle their money. I advised him to find a regular job . . . as a salesman, whatever."

"He had no other sources of revenue?"

"No."

DeKok nodded slowly to himself, ignoring the exciting sight of the woman, panting with indignation. Vledder noted with interest the curves of her body, clearly outlined by the tight-fitting dress.

A sad smile played around DeKok's lips as he urged her to sit down. When she was again seated, he gestured around the room, pointing at the walls and the expensive furniture.

"So, all these years you have both lived off the proceeds of crime. All of this," his voice sounded bitter, "and his countless dissipations have been financed with the money cheerfully donated by people who contributed devoutly, believing the funds to be for missionaries and to help relieve the suffering of others."

She seemed to shrink in her chair.

"But there was nothing I could do," she complained. "What could I have done. When I married Richard I thought he was a well-to-do businessman. When I finally realized how he accumulated his money, there was no way out. Richard wasn't the sort of man who could live in poverty."

DeKok snorted contemptuously.

"But you could have."

Monique Vankerk did not answer. She bowed her head, hiding her face.

DeKok stood up and looked down at her. The interview had exposed her, had taken away the magical aura created by her undeniable beauty. The beauty was still there, but the enchantment had disappeared.

He strolled around the room and looked at the paintings. Among the painting he discovered what he believed to be a John Constable and a Ruysdael. Constable was one of the classics and Ruysdael was considered the landscape equivalent of Rembrandt. He wondered if the paintings were copies. Even if just those two were genuine, they represented a considerable capital.

He went back to the chair and sat down again.

"Do you remember when you last spoke to Richard?"

Monique Vankerk lifted her head from her arms. Tears glistened in her eyes.

"When . . . when he . . . when he left home for the last time."

"You have to speak the truth."

She licked her lips.

"I'm telling the truth."

DeKok shook his head.

"No. The last time you spoke to him was by telephone. You were in Cortina d'Ampezzo at the time."

Her eyes became big and scared.

"You . . . you *know* that?"

The old Inspector nodded calmly.

"And I know a lot more." He looked at her evenly. "You were sharing the apartment with Brother Rigobertus, a man who, as supreme leader of the Community of Brothers and Sisters of the Holy Blessings, had been sworn to a chaste and moral life."

Monique closed her eyes. She paled. She released a deep sigh.

"Brother Rigobertus was, *is* a dear, sweet, *gentle* man. A relief . . . after Richard."

DeKok nodded.

"How long have you had a relationship with him?"

She stroked her forehead, as if trying to get rid of a headache.

"A few months. Sometimes it was a burden for us, both of us. We constantly had to control ourselves. We could not afford to let our relationship be known . . . especially within the Community. Our, our . . . *love*, had to remain hidden."

DeKok pulled on his lower lip and let it plop back. He repeated the annoying gesture several times.

"So," he said finally, "that's why you fled to Cortina from time to time." He was speculating and could only hope to guess right. As if it was a foregone conclusion, he continued. "And there you were spotted by the Shoebeeks who happened to be on vacation in the same area, at the same time."

She seemed to hesitate, willing to deny. Then she slowly nodded her head in agreement.

"We had been skiing that day," she said slowly, "and we were resting in the bar. Suddenly they came in and walked straight toward us. There was no way out, no way to hide. It was inevitable."

DeKok stood up and leaned over her.

"And then, after a few casual remarks, Mrs. Shoebeek started to talk about chastity and morality and promised to call a special meeting of the Brothers and Sisters. You then realized you had to act quickly."

She seemed to shrink further away and gave him a frightened look.

"I . . . I . . . don't . . . I don't know what you mean," she stammered.

DeKok grinned crookedly, a gleam of triumph in his eyes.

121

"Monique Vankerk ... I accuse you ... and Brother Rigobertus ... of the murder of Mr. and Mrs. Shoebeek ... followed by the murders of Richard Vankerk and Blonde Tina."

11

"No, *no*, NO!"

DeKok sighed. These wild denials were becoming a staple of his career. He watched Monique calmly as she screamed unrestrainedly at him. "We didn't do it!" She sprang out of the chair. "We could *never* have done it. Brother Rigobertus would not be *capable* of doing such a thing. He's much too, too *good* for that. He's the gentlest man I've ever met in my life. She stared at the gray sleuth. Her eyes were dilated, her nostrils flared, she gestured wildly with both hands. "*Murder* . . . how can you *think* such a thing of us?"

DeKok merely shrugged his shoulders.

"Murder isn't just obscene, it is also an entirely *human* business. I've known some of the *gentlest* . . ." His tone was ironic. " . . . murderers," he concluded.

She let herself fall back in her chair and looked up at him with a pale face. Tears had ruined her make-up. Black streaks of mascara covered her cheeks. She shook her head.

"You *must* believe me! Brother Rigobertus and I are innocent."

DeKok looked impassive.

"How did your husband know he could reach you in Cortina?"

I told him, of course. He always knew where I was."

DeKok's eyebrows made one of those impossible, improbable movements. For a brief moment they actually looked as if they were floating in front of his forehead. Then the movement subsided as quickly as it had begun. Neither Vledder, nor Monique had noticed anything. Monique was too upset to notice much of anything and Vledder was intent on watching her reactions to DeKok's words.

"Did your husband know about your . . . eh, your . . . affair with Rigobertus?"

Monique shook her head slowly.

"I never told him. I don't think he knew about it." She paused, barely suppressing a sob. "He never made any allusions to it."

DeKok gave her a searching look.

"Then . . . *how* did you explain your frequent trips across the border?"

She glanced at him from under long lashes. A little color had come back in her cheeks.

"I negotiated them with Richard."

"Negotiated? In exchange for what?"

She lowered her head and nodded.

"In . . . in exchange for . . . love."

DeKok's laugh was sarcastic.

"Otherwise you'd lock the door of your bedroom," he declared.

She nodded again and sighed.

"That," she answered slowly, softly, "is what it amounted to. I told Richard that life with him was unbearable, unless I could take time off, from time to time."

DeKok snorted. His puritanical soul rebelled at the thought of that type of arrangement. It was, in his opinion disgusting and, above all, dishonest. Strangely enough, he never felt the same way about the relationships between a prostitute and her clients. In his mind they were straightforward, honest business relationships.

He pursed his lips in thought, then asked the next question.

"And then you left for some kind of hotel across the border and Brother Rigobertus followed you faithfully?"

"That's the way it happened, yes."

"And Richard always knew where you were?"

"Yes, he did."

DeKok smiled suddenly.

"Weren't you afraid he might follow you? Then it would all be over . . . your affair with Rigobertus exposed."

She smiled sadly in return.

"Richard was much too busy with his own affairs. He literally overflowed with virility. Apparently even in the Community of the Brothers and Sisters there have been incidents that were later covered up."

"What sort of things?"

"Messing around with girls and young women."

The gray sleuth fell back in his chair. The interview had taken more of a toll than he cared to admit. He glanced at Vledder, who immediately understood the silent hint. Vledder leaned closer to Monique.

"Why did Richard call you in Cortina?" asked the young man.

She rubbed her face, spreading the mascara on her cheeks.

"About our eventual divorce. He said that he had come to a definitive decision and had decided to marry Tina, He had taken money from the bank and told me he would not return here . . . to our home, here at Brewers Canal."

"Was that all?"

She hesitated, wrung her hands and then dropped them in her lap.

"Richard also asked if I insisted on my conditions for a divorce, that is, that he would resign as treasurer of the Carillon."

Vledder drummed his fingers on the arm of his chair.

"Well, and?" he asked when she remained silent.

She nodded slowly.

"I told him in no uncertain terms that I had not changed my mind. I would not agree to a divorce, unless he resigned."

"How did he react to *that*?"

"He cursed and broke the connection."

Vledder scratched the back of his neck. Then he gestured in her direction.

"Was Brother Rigobertus in the room with you when the call came through? Could he hear the conversation?"

"I think so, he was standing right next to me."

Vledder raised a finger in the air and looked at it as if he had never seen it before. When he realized he was imitating one of DeKok's mannerism, he flushed slightly and lowered his hand hastily.

"So he knew that Richard was committing fraud, was cheating the Community?"

"He had known for some time." She nodded resignedly.

"How did he find out?"

"I told him."

Vledder seemed surprised. He frowned.

"And he allowed it?"

She shook her head emphatically.

"No, of course not! Rigobertus was looking for a solution . . . an *elegant* solution, a solution that would not undermine the faith of the members."

Vledder grinned.

"So that the source of the funds would not be affected."

Monique Vankerk rose from her chair.

126

"I'm not a member of the Carillon," she said apologetically. "I cannot be held responsible for policy." She walked to a mirror on the near wall and looked at the ruins of her make-up. With a minuscule handkerchief she wiped away the traces of mascara and used her hands to rearrange her hair. She seemed more in control of herself, more sure of herself after the shocks DeKok had given her. She turned her back on the mirror and walked back to her chair. Gracefully she sat down and crossed her legs. Her dress hiked up her thigh and showed an alarming amount of shapely leg, encased in black stockings without garters. The narrow strip of pale skin between the top of the stocking and the hem of the dress created an extra titillation. But at this time both men were immune to the temptation of her beauty.

"You must remember," she said coolly, "that the Community supports a number of charitable organizations."

Vledder gave her a sharp look.

"So, if I understand what you're saying, the death of the treasurer was not exactly unwelcome to Brother Rigobertus."

She reacted angrily.

"He had nothing to do with Richard's death!" she cried out.

Vledder grinned a crooked grin.

"And of course," he continued blandly, "the death of the Shoebeeks could also be considered one of the ... Holy Blessings."

Monique's face became a mask. A fire glowed in her green eyes.

"Brother Rigobertus had already considered the consequences of their discovery. When Mrs. Shoebeek threatened to expose us during a special meeting, he said that, for love of me, he was prepared to resign his leadership position in the Community."

"But yet they died," said Vledder with an ironic bow in her direction.

Monique Vankerk looked at the young Inspector as if he was something that had crawled from under a rock. Then her face softened slightly and as Vledder marveled at the range of emotions that fled across her face, she suddenly looked scared.

"B-b-brother C-c-crispin," she stammered, visibly upset. "He was the only one who knew."

* * *

Silently they walked along the edge of Brewers Canal and then via Gentlemen's Canal toward Harlem Street. The old, square building of the former West-Indian Company looked dilapidated after the damage caused by a recent fire. It was here that the onetime contemporary of Drake, the pirate Piet Hein, now generally revered as a national hero about whom songs were sung, had displayed the treasures he had stolen with his capture of the Spanish Silver Fleet. The "Seventeen Gentlemen", after which the Gentlemen's Canal is named and who led the East- and West Indian Companies at the time, were very much impressed. But for once, neither DeKok, nor Vledder, gave the building a second thought. This time they were not interested in the past, but in the present.

Monique had given them a lot to think about.

Vledder finally broke the silence.

"You were in top, form," he said with admiration. "A good interview. I especially liked the way you stated as fact that the Shoebeeks had seen Monique and her lover in Cortina. An inspired guess. Monique didn't even bother to deny it. She just assumed you knew all about it. Considering that the couple died, she could have easily denied everything." He paused and looked at his mentor. "How did you know that Brother Rigobertus had sworn an oath of chastity?"

"Didn't you know?"

128

Vledder shook his head.

"The Brother I talked to, didn't say a thing about that."

DeKok smiled.

"But it was very simple. After I had sent you for information, I asked my wife to call the Community with a request for information. She told them that she had an acquaintance who was already a member, that she contemplated joining as well."

"And?"

DeKok grinned boyishly.

"They sent her a beautiful brochure."

Vledder grimaced.

"And in that you read that the leader of the Community had to swear an oath of morality and chastity."

"Exactly. It was described as a sacrifice on the part of Brother Rigobertus in order to allow him to better attend to his important duties on behalf of the Brothers and Sisters . . . to lead them toward ultimate happiness."

"But why chastity?"

"Well, apparently it's all right for the leader of the Community to be married, there is no vow of abstinence, as with Catholic priests, you understand . . . just chastity . . . 'cleave only unto her,' as in the wedding vows."

Vledder snorted.

"Why don't they just say: No hanky-panky? As if that would have made much of a difference . . . he certainly was less than chaste with Monique."

DeKok rubbed the bridge of his nose.

"Ach, my boy, it's only human . . . in a way I can appreciate that."

Vledder gaped at him.

"You mean to tell me that it won't be a motive for murder?"

DeKok looked thoughtful.

129

"The accusation you raised against Monique was cleverly deducted. I listened with pleasure. But it was not exactly air-tight. There are a number of . . . eh, *practical* considerations."

"Such as?"

"Time, for one. Somebody must have had the time to commit the murders."

Vledder gave his old friend a suspicious look.

"And Monique and Rigobertus lacked the time?"

At the end of Harlem Street, in the center of the bridge across the Singel, DeKok stopped and leaned his elbows on the railing. With an appreciative eye he looked out over the open Harbor Front, actually the inner harbor of Amsterdam, and at the striking architecture of the Central Station. He found a stick of chewing gum in one of his pockets. He unwrapped it and dutifully put the paper back in his pocket, rather than polluting the canal. Then he put the stick in his mouth and turned toward Vledder.

Vledder stood next to him, waiting for an answer.

"Well," urged the young man finally, "*did* they have the time?"

"You said yourself," said DeKok, "that both double murders have the same signature . . . clearly committed by the same perpetrator, or perpetrators. The victims, all four of them, have been found drowned in an Amsterdam Canal. When we checked on the telephone calls, we found that at the time that Richard had called Monique, the Shoebeeks, still very much alive, had already left Italy. But, you see, Monique and Rigobertus were still in Italy. Therefore it seems a bit forced to accuse those two of the murder of the Shoebeeks. There simply was no time. There's also a time problem with the murder of Richard and Blonde Tina. Just think about it a moment . . . both disappeared on the first of February. That was the day Richard called Monique, who was still in Italy."

The young Inspector stared at the water below.

"I'm afraid," he said somberly, "that you're right . . . again."

DeKok smiled.

"But that doesn't mean I have excluded either as a suspect."

"Eh?"

DeKok raised a finger in the air and spoke in a didactic tone of voice.

"There does remain another possibility."

"Oh, yes? What, then?"

DeKok used the raised finger to rub the bridge of his nose. Then he looked at it for several seconds before lowering his hand back on the railing of the bridge. Vledder had a brief feeling of *deja vu*, when he realized he had made more or less the same gestures himself, not too long ago.

DeKok seemed unaware of what went trough Vledder's mind.

"Let us assume," continued the gray sleuth, "that Brother Rigobertus lied . . . let's say that he was not, how did Monique say that? That he was *not* prepared, out of love for her, to resign his position in the Community. He would have had time to follow the Shoebeeks from Italy and kill them almost immediately after their arrival in Amsterdam."

Vledder waved his arms in protest.

"But . . . but on the first of February he was still in Cortina d'Ampezzo!"

"How do you know that?" asked DeKok, a grin on his face.

"Monique told us . . . Monique told us that Rigobertus was standing right next to her when Richard called."

"And?"

"What . . . and?"

DeKok gave his young friend a penetrating look.

"If Monique lied . . . on purpose . . . to provide Rigobertus with a perfect alibi?'

"You mean," said Vledder, stating the obvious as was his wont, "that he could have been in Amsterdam . . . not in Cortina?"

"Exactly."

The young man paled.

"But that means . . . that means he could also have killed Richard Vankerk and Blonde Tina!"

DeKok let go of the bridge railing and walked away.

"That's it exactly, my boy," he said in a tired voice. "That's it in a nutshell."

From the busy New Dike they walked toward Old Bridge Alley and back to the Damrak. Young Vledder looked petulant. He had the uneasy feeling that, as usual, he had either missed something, or let himself be swayed by his own enthusiasm. He stared at the herring man and wondered if DeKok planned to eat another herring, or two. But DeKok passed by without giving the herring stand another look. Of course, grumbled Vledder to himself, why should he ever be predictable. It was a recurring theme, he thought. He had worked with DeKok for several years now, but he never really understood the older man. At decisive moments DeKok reminded him more of a magician, than a cop. The old man had a habit of pulling the rabbit out of the hat, without seeming to be aware of the hat, or the rabbit.

"How are we going to prove it?" asked Vledder, unable to remain silent any longer.

"What?"

"That Brother Rigobertus *was* in Amsterdam at the time."

"That's not going to be easy," admitted DeKok. "Unless Monique changes her mind and decides to tell us the truth."

"Do you think she will?"

"Not really," said DeKok, shaking his head slowly. "If we're unable to find something to exert some . . . pressure on her, then . . ." He did not complete the sentence, but climbed the steps toward the entrance of the age-old police station at Warmoes Street.

Meindert Post, the current Watch Commander looked up from behind his desk.

"So," he roared in his normal speaking voice, "there you are . . . finally!"

DeKok walked closer.

"Were you looking for us?"

Post grinned.

"Always the same story," he laughed, "you can never find a cop when you want one."

DeKok looked innocent.

"But isn't that the purpose of the police," he asked, "not to be there when they're wanted?"

They laughed together.

Meindert Post pointed at the notes on his desk.

"All kidding aside," he said, "Little Lowee was here. He wanted to talk to you about . . . sex."

"Lowee? About sex?" DeKok was dumbfounded.

Post shrugged his shoulders.

"Perhaps he's in sex-education," he laughed. "Anyway," he continued, "there's a religious person waiting for you upstairs."

"What's that supposed to mean?"

"A Brother," explained Post.

"Brother?"

"Yes," said Post, consulting his notes, "a Brother Crispin."

133

12

The slender young man was seated on the bench outside the detective room. DeKok held the door and motioned the man inside. The man was dressed in an expensive black suit, a white shirt and a pearl-gray tie. His hair was short and blond and in his eyes was the look of a person driven by certainties. There were no questions in his life, thought Vledder, he knows all the answers and if you don't believe it, just ask him.

Before entering the room, the man stretched out his hand to DeKok.

"Crispin," he said in a cheery voice, "Brother Crispin of the Community of the Brothers and Sisters of the Holy Blessings, at your service."

DeKok shook the offered hand.

"Let's go to my desk," he said.

After they were seated, DeKok addressed Crispin.

"A waning Community, to be sure."

Brother Crispin showed surprise.

"Waning?"

"Yes. After the sorrowful departure of Mr. and Mrs. Shoebeek, you have also recently lost Brother Christian from your ranks."

Brother Crispin bowed his head.

"May God keep him."

"God and the Devil . . . they each get their share." DeKok spread his hands on the desk. "But I, I don't get my share . . . I miss out."

"How do you miss out?"

"I miss out on the killer . . . the murderer."

Brother Crispin's face sobered.

"Yes," he sighed. "I have heard that you suspect murder. Brother Rigobertus was very much upset about it. He hopes and prays that you will change your views in the course of the investigation." For the first time he looked DeKok full in the face. "Is it really murder?" he asked.

DeKok nodded emphatically.

"Two double murders."

Brother Crispin seemed to compose himself and folded his hands devoutly.

"I . . . and many of the Brothers and Sisters of the Community, do not agree with you. We are convinced that they, the dear departed, were no longer able to face the burden of life."

DeKok cocked his head.

"Simple suicide?"

"Simple . . . yes."

"And that is why you ordered them cremated."

Brother Crispin did not answer at once. He stared past DeKok at nothing at all, avoided eye contact.

"According to the tenets of our beliefs," the Brother said finally, "we, in the Community, feel that those who slay themselves have lost all rights to a Christian burial." He gestured apologetically. "My function within the Carillon is to make sure that the purity of our beliefs remain inviolate. That is why I recommended cremation."

DeKok leaned closer. He felt close to losing his temper. The salving, self-righteous voice of the other irritated him greatly.

"Alberdina Tuijlinga, Blonde Tina in the vernacular and a dear friend of mine, was *not* a member of your Community. Whatever made you insists that she be cremated?"

The smooth, calculated gestures of Brother Crispin lost some of their self-assurance.

"I told the old, lame woman who professed to be her mother," he said with unctuous satisfaction, ". . . that we should not separate those whom God had united in death."

There was a dangerous light in DeKok's eyes and Vledder held himself in readiness to intervene. It was not unknown for DeKok to go off into a berserker rage when confronted with smug stupidity. But the moment passed.

"So you burned them both," snorted DeKok, "to give them a taste of the Hell that awaited them."

Brother Crispin lost some more of his poise.

"That is no way to speak of cremation."

DeKok pressed his lips together and glared at the man. Then he burst out:

"But that's nevertheless the way it is," he yelled. "In your eyes . . . in your damned vanity you take it upon yourself to sit on God's throne and judge those who do not happen to conform to your precious, stilted concepts of what is right and wrong."

Vledder realized that DeKok had used 'damned' not as a swear word, but in a religious sense. He looked with wonder at his partner. DeKok had always struck him as a thoroughly *good* man, a just man. But he had never suspected him of being a religious fanatic.

DeKok reached across the desk and grabbed the smug Brother Crispin by the lapels of his beautiful, expensive suit jacket. He pulled the man closer. The fear on the face of Crispin did nothing to cool off DeKok.

"I'll tell you why you insisted that your victims be cremated," hissed DeKok, close to the others's face. "You knew very well they had been murdered. You knew that from the very start. And you were also quite aware that the motives for the murders were to be found within your own, precious Community. And *that* is why . . . in order to preserve the precious *purity* of your beliefs . . . you realized that cremation was the perfect solution to nullify any incriminating evidence."

With a contemptuous gesture DeKok released the man. Vledder quickly supported him and guided him back in his chair. With one eye on Crispin and another eye on DeKok, Vledder smoothed out the man's ruffled clothes and at the same time gave his old partner a warning glance.

DeKok stood at the other side of the desk, breathing heavily. His broad face no longer looked like a good-natured boxer, but more like an angry mastiff. He looked down on Crispin, noting with part of his mind that Vledder had again stepped back. Behind DeKok's angry face his mind was calm and working at full capacity. He was determined to break through the facade of arrogant self-importance of his opponent.

Brother Crispin collected himself as best he could. Sweat beaded his forehead and his hands shook as he adjusted his shirt cuffs. DeKok's sudden attack had definitely shaken him. There was a hint of fear in his eyes when he looked up at the old cop.

"You," he tried, "you . . . you don't have the right to treat me this way." He shook his head as if to clear it. "I shall complain to your superiors regarding your behavior."

DeKok shrugged.

"Please do," he said. Then he leaned closer and Crispin involuntarily seemed to shrink back in his chair. "But I'm still waiting for an answer to my question," insisted DeKok.

Brother Crispin sighed. His face was pale and there was still a haunted look in his eyes.

"Our leader, Brother Rigobertus, has sent me here to explain anything you might want to know. Within our Community . . . among ourselves, there are no disagreements so great that they could lead to murder." He swallowed. "And to answer your reckless, foolish accusations . . . my decision to have the victims cremated was based solely on religious grounds and certainly had nothing to do with any attempt to . . . eh, to destroy . . . incriminating evidence, as you called it." He sat up straight in an attempt to regain some control of the conversation. "At the very least you will have to *prove* your accusation."

DeKok sat down behind his desk. He looked intently at Crispin, studied him. Obviously the man was a formidable opponent. The gray sleuth rubbed his face in a tired gesture. When he pulled down his hands, his face had a different expression: milder, more receptive.

"Mr. and Mrs. Shoebeek," he said in a friendly tone of voice, "wrote you a letter wherein they requested a special meeting."

"Yes, they did."

"Do you still have the letter?"

Brother Crispin shook his head.

"I destroyed it. After their death it served no purpose to follow up on their request."

"How efficient," smiled DeKok.

"What do you mean?"

DeKok made a gesture, indicating disinterest.

"Your destruction of the letter. Now there's nobody left to prove what the Shoebeeks told you in the letter . . . that is, that they reported to you that they had seen Brother Rigobertus in Cortina, accompanied by the beautiful wife of another member of the Carillon, the late Brother Christian."

Brother Crispin seemed genuinely confused. His nostrils quivered delicately. He moved his head from side to side and Vledder expected him to rake his hair with his hands.

"No . . . no, that is not true at all."

DeKok rose from his chair. Slowly he stretched out an accusing finger toward Brother Crispin.

"You knew," he said calmly, "about the discovery the Shoebeeks had made during their vacation. You also knew what the implications were if that discovery were to be revealed to the entire membership. It would mean the total disavowal of your leader, Brother Rigobertus, the man with whom you feel a bond. He said it himself: Brother Crispin . . . a great comfort, my right hand . . . devout, dedicated."

DeKok lowered his accusing hand and leaned both hands on his desk. He leaned closer to the Brother.

"In order to protect *him*, in order to preserve the unity within the Community, to protect the *purity* of your beliefs . . . you decided on a desperate measure . . . murder."

Brother Crispin stared at DeKok. His eyes were wide. He slid from the chair and kneeled down in prayer.

"Dear Lord," he besieged, "please abide with me now that Evil is nigh."

* * *

Vledder looked at his old mentor with a broad grin on his face.

"I *like* that Brother Crispin," exclaimed the young man. "Finally a man who manages to typify you exactly: DeKok . . . Evil that is nigh."

DeKok stared somberly out of the window. Either he had not heard Vledder's remark, or could not appreciate it. His face remained expressionless as he stared out over the rooftops, rocking slightly on the balls of his feet.

Vledder concluded that DeKok was discontented. DeKok's thoughts echoed his partner's opinion. He was totally dissatisfied with the progress of the case. It seemed that at every turn he found himself confronted with a wall, a wall as high as that around the temple in Duivendrecht, a wall of lies, obstructionism, disappearing evidence and utter frustration.

After several minutes he turned around and started to pace up and down the large, busy detective room. Without visible effort he avoided all obstacles and people in his path. The difficulty, he thought, is the absence of a fitting motive. His theories were based on reality, but he could not shake the feeling that he missed something, something essential, something that would uncover a carefully hidden, dark secret.

He stopped in front of Vledder's desk.

"I'm pretty well convinced that Brother Crispin knew the reason for the request by the Shoebeeks. There must have been at least a hint about it in the letter they wrote. Also ..." DeKok leaned his hands on Vledder's desk, grimaced and then went on: "Probably the only thing Monique said that had the ring of truth, is that Brother Crispin knew about them. The question remains, however, what did he do with that knowledge? I feel that the most likely reaction would have been to confront Brother Rigobertus at the earliest opportunity."

Vledder looked pensive.

"Granted," he said, "but then he had to know where to find Rigobertus ... must have known how to reach him. And that would mean ... that he also knew about the relationship between Monique and Rigobertus."

DeKok nodded agreement.

"Very good. But it's also possible that Brother Rigobertus contacted Crispin, immediately after meeting the Shoebeeks in the bar in Cortina. That would also mean that Crispin was already informed, *before* he received the letter. Any which way you twist it . . . it's obvious that some sort of agreement has been reached between Crispin and his spiritual leader, Rigobertus."

Vledder looked up at him.

"Murder?"

DeKok looked annoyed.

"The Shoebeeks' knowledge did not just pose a threat to Rigobertus, the leader of the Community, but to the entire group. A fanatic like Crispin would have considered murder an acceptable alternative." He paused, straightened out and stretched himself. "Up to that point my instinct and my reasoning seem to agree. But what about the murder of Richard Vankerk and Blonde Tina? What were the motives in *that* case. Did they also pose a threat to the . . . eh, the *purity* of the faith? A purity that is close to Crispin's heart?" DeKok shook his head, answering his own questions. "No," he said in an irritated voice, "that's not it. It's something else."

Suddenly he turned around and walked to the coat rack. Vledder followed him hastily.

"Where are you going?"

DeKok grinned a boyish grin, transforming his face as if the sun had come out.

"I'm off to Lowee's. Perhaps his spirits will revive mine."

13

Little Lowee hastily wiped his hands on his apron. He watched DeKok as the detective hoisted himself on his favorite barstool.

"I was gonna see ya at the station," said Lowee, "but you was gone, they tole me."

DeKok nodded calmly.

"That's right," he admitted. He looked at the small barkeeper with some suspicion in his eyes. "It must have been really important."

"Whadda you mean?"

"You don't normally like to come to the station voluntarily."

Little Lowee grimaced.

"Ah, well . . . I don't wanna let everybody know I likes you."

DeKok smiled, flattered.

"I have never heard you express it just this way."

Lowee made a nonchalant gesture.

"You knows what I thinks . . . without you guys the inner city woulda been inna bigger mess already, what with all them druggies and other garbage." He held up a bottle of fine cognac. "Same recipe?"

Without waiting for an answer he dived under the bar and emerged with three large snifters. Carefully he placed the glasses on the bar and poured generously.

"I knows," the barkeeper said conversationally while pouring, "That you guys are still worrying about them stiffs you fished out of Emperors Canal." He glanced quickly around the bar. "This week there was a broad in the bar. She tole me she'd known Uncle Rickie real good . . . said he was some kinda bigwig inna religious something or other."

"What kind of woman?"

"You knows, justa working girl. She said she'd been a member of that group, but now she's back inna business. Wasn't that much different from what she's been doing, nohow, she said."

DeKok frowned.

"You mean between that religious organization and the Red Light District?"

Lowee shrugged his narrow shoulders.

"Exactum. That's what she says."

"Then what?"

Lowee pushed the glasses in front of his guests and took his own by the delicate stem. None of the men attempted to take the first sip. Lowee was too full of news and Vledder and DeKok were too curious to hear what the small barkeeper had to say.

"I tole her that you guys thought it was sorta strange that Uncle Rickie had drowned. But she says, that ain't no mystery, they shoulda killed him long ago. And then I says, how come? And she says, that guy's brains were in 'is crotch."

"A strange place," remarked DeKok, eyes narrowed.

The small barkeeper laughed heartily.

"Come off it, DeKok, she means to say the guy only thinks of sex, you see. Tha' was all he thunk about. Tha's what I tole them at the station, itsa bout sex."

DeKok nodded thoughtfully.

"Did she say anything else?"

Lowee shook his head.

"You gotta watch it, you knows. I dinna want her to feel I was after info. That woulna be safe. I never seen her before, you knows. I just let it slide."

DeKok bit his lower lip.

"I would have liked to talk to her myself."

Little Lowee chirruped. The beady eyes in his small, mousey face gleamed with pleasure.

"I knows it," he exclaimed, "I says to meself, DeKok wanna talk to this broad. Tha's why I tell her to go see Greta. Tha's where she be. Now that Tina is dead, Lame Greta gotta room left."

DeKok raised his glass, laughing.

"*Proost*," he said cynically, "to crime and prostitution."

Lowee nodded seriously.

"And to all the children of thirsty fathers," he added.

Vledder remained silent.

* * *

Lame Greta pushed slices of an orange between the bars of the canary cage. She made shushing sounds and talked endearments to her little feathered friend. She looked around when DeKok walked in.

"What more do you want?" she asked, irritation in her voice. "Are you going to keep on bothering me. Am I never to be rid of you?"

DeKok gave her a winning smile. He understood her completely.

"You can expect me to keep coming back," he said reasonably, "until I have found the killer of your Tina."

She nodded, her face even.

"I should have known. After all these years, I should have known. You would put pressure on your own mother, if you thought she held the key to a solution."

DeKok shook his head sadly.

"My old mother would give me the key right-a-way ... without pressure." He smiled. "But I'm not here for you. I wanted to talk to your new girl."

"Anna?"

"Is that her name?"

"Yes, Blonde Anna."

"Sound like Blonde Tina."

There was a wild look in her eyes when she answered.

"Tina was my child."

DeKok placed a comforting arm around her bony shoulders.

"Why did you take in a new girl?"

"I must have somebody to take care of."

"And to earn money for you."

She rubbed the table cloth with an absent-minded gesture.

"I never got that much out of Tina. She needed so much for herself."

"Sure, sure," soothed DeKok. Then, after a brief pause: "You mind calling Anna for me?" He paused again. "Did you know she knew Rickie?"

The old woman rose from her chair and sighed.

"I think, in retrospect, that I may have made a terrible mistake. Rickie wasn't the man I thought he was at all." She shook her head dejectedly. "You should never judge a person by exteriors."

She closed the door behind her and shuffled away. DeKok listened to the slapping sound of her slippers on the stairs.

146

A few minutes later she came in, a young, blonde prostitute with a fine figure and a face with too much make-up. She was dressed in a wrap-a-round housecoat and high-heeled slippers. DeKok knew she would be naked under the housecoat, but it did not affect him. He was used to the ways of the neighborhood and the way some of the younger whores tried to shock him.

He pulled out a chair for her, realizing he did not know her, had never seen her before. She sat down, showing an unnecessary amount of leg and breast.

"I heard," said DeKok, seating himself across from her, "That you used to belong to the Community of Brothers and Sisters of the Holy Blessings." He looked at her slender figure and smiled encouragingly. "How did that happen?"

She pulled the coat tighter around herself, covering her cleavage.

"I was brought up in a Christian household, reformed protestant. After I had been in the Life for a while, I met a nice client, an older gentleman . . . he became a regular. He was a member of the Community. He said that I lived a life of sin and that the Brothers and Sisters of the Community would understand my return to the Lord."

"And that's when you became a member?"

She nodded, hesitated.

"Not at once. First I went to a few services in the temple. That was impressive. There was singing and preaching. It was a lot like when I was a kid when I used to go to church with my father."

DeKok nodded fatherly. He gave her another good look. When he looked behind the make-up he saw a sweet, but dumb face.

"Surely you got some benefit from it."

She moved in her chair. One breast fell out of the opening of her coat. With a routine, careless gesture she pushed it back under the material and covered it.

"Yes, I did. Suddenly I realized that, as a working girl, I lived a life of sin. Shortly thereafter I quit. I lived for a few months with my old john. It was a good time . . . really. He was very nice to me and I didn't have to do a lot for him. Just occasionally . . . you know. The poor dear was hardly capable anymore. Mostly he just liked to look. Anyway, on his advice I had myself baptized."

"But you were already baptized, weren't you?"

"Yes, in the reformed protestant church. But this time I had myself baptized in the temple."

"With the Brothers and Sisters?"

"Yes. In the baptismal basin. Brother Rigobertus baptized me himself. It was quite an honor. I have also . . ."

DeKok raised his hand to interrupt.

"I've been in the temple, but I didn't see a baptismal font, let alone a basin."

She shrugged, causing the housecoat to fall open again. With an impatient gesture she covered herself.

"It's exactly in the center. Under the floor. During normal services the basin is covered. When there are baptizing ceremonies, the floor moves aside and all the Brothers and Sisters sit around the basin."

"As in your case?"

"Oh, yes," she nodded with sparkling eyes. "it was really nice. They were all there . . . except those who were too ill to come. I've never really regretted it, in a way. I had a good life after the baptizing. The Brothers and Sisters were always very good to me."

DeKok spread his hands in astonishment.

"Then why did you leave?"

She smiled a bitter smile.

"When the respected members of the Carillon took a good look at my . . ., eh, . . . my charms, I was often invited to receive special blessings."

"Oh, and what did that mean?"

She raised a leg from under her housecoat and looked at it critically. Then she smiled at DeKok.

"There were exhaustive discussions about my sinful past. I had to explain exactly what a working girl, I mean a whore . . . they always insisted on that word, what I did for a living. You know, what my customers wanted from me. Often it would end in a demonstration."

"For the members of the Carillon?"

She grimaced.

"Yes. In a way I didn't mind. I have a good body, I'm not ashamed of it and . . . I'm used to this and that." She looked up at DeKok, who suddenly realized that the vacuity in her face was not so much dullness, as innocence. "Anyway," she continued, "I thought that it was part of the rituals, part of my reformation, so to speak."

DeKok grinned mirthlessly.

"Sex as purification of sins."

She nodded slowly, as if realizing for the first time how ridiculous it sounded.

"Yes, actually. They *did* make it seem like a religious rite, you know. As if it were a privilege. As if it were a blessing and they wanted to share their happiness with me."

DeKok gave her a searching look.

"Is it still that way?"

She sighed.

"That I don't know, exactly. You see, ever since Brother Castor resigned from the Carillon, I've not been invited for special blessings in the temple."

"But that's more than a month ago."

She nodded again. Her tongue flicked out and wet her lips.

"It took a while for me to wake up, to realize they had played me for a sap. I realized that the leaders of the Community were untrustworthy, dirty hypocrites. That's when I finally made the break. I thought to myself that if this was the way I had to take religion, I'd be better off going back to the business." She made the universal movement of rubbing her thumb and index finger together, as if paying out coins. "At least I get paid," she added.

DeKok stared at her in total amazement. Then, on impulse, he covered her hands with his. It was not a melodramatic, or theatrical gesture.

"My dear child," he said sincerely, "my sincere best wishes and all my blessings." He shook his gray head. "And for that you don't have to go to bed with me."

He stood up and followed by Vledder, who had remained in the background, he left, leaving a bemused prostitute behind.

* * *

From Rear Fort Canal they walked back to Warmoes Street. Vledder glanced at his mentor, who shuffled along, head bent, deep in thought.

"You believe it?"

DeKok looked at him, gathering his thought.

"What?"

"About the extra blessings. I have a feeling it's nothing but lies."

"Why is that?"

Vledder gestured impatiently.

"You've been around a lot longer than I, surely you know those young whores . . . untrustworthy and always ready to blow something out of proportion, make it sensational."

DeKok rubbed the back of his neck.

"A nice generality and therefore, of course, suspect. But you're right, it's a sensational story, well suited to anybody's imagination, not just that of a prostitute. In this case, however, I'd like to keep in mind that Monique Vankerk *also* spoke about 'messing around with girls and young women' and that gives food for thought."

Vledder objected.

"But only in regard to Richard Vankerk. If we believe Blonde Anna, *all* the members of the Carillon are extremely, how do I say it, sex-oriented."

DeKok glanced aside, a painful look on his face.

"I broke off the interrogation too soon. I should have asked Anna to identify the specific members of the Carillon who were so interested in extra blessings." He paused, waved a hand in return to the greeting from some petty criminal, then continued: "I also found it significant that the invitations to Anna ceased, after Brother Castor had resigned from the Carillon."

"Perhaps she was no longer in fashion," shrugged Vledder. "Maybe they were tired of her and were looking for somebody new."

"Aha, now you seem to believe it after all."

"Well, I mean . . ."

"I feel," interrupted DeKok, "that it's more a matter of something else. For instance, what if Mrs. Shoebeek had found out something like that, about a month ago, and had given the gentlemen an ultimatum. One of the conditions being, of course, that her husband resigned from the Carillon. Perhaps that scared the others . . . at least forced them to be more circumspect."

Vledder laughed.

"So, they're just 'resting' as they say in the theater, until the performances can begin again."

DeKok did not answer. He walked into the station, walked past the Watch Commander and climbed the stairs to the next floor. Vledder followed close behind.

When they entered the detective room, Vledder was just in time to intercept a colleague from answering the phone on DeKok's desk. The young inspector took the receiver and listened. He looked at DeKok and then, with a pale face, replaced the receiver on the instrument.

"We . . . we must go back to Emperors Canal."

"What's up."

Vledder panted.

"A municipal dredger has just brought two corpses to the surface."

DeKok was visibly upset.

"Who?"

Vledder swallowed.

"Not sure, but sounds like Brother Rigobertus and Monique Vankerk."

14

Inspector DeKok jumped, with a suppleness that belied his years, from the high side of the canal onto the deck of the barge and from there moved to the wet and slippery deck of the dredger. The two corpses had been placed side by side next to the diagonally rising bucket "ladder" of the dredger. The skipper had not separated the bodies. The arms were still entwined and the fingers were tightly wrapped around each other.

He looked at the two corpses. From his viewpoint the scene looked peaceful, intimate, as if the two dead people had decided to interrupt a happy stroll by stepping into the hereafter. DeKok shook his head. The impression was illusionary, a sham, a macabre attempt to present violent death in an idyllic setting. The old Inspector snorted, a grim expression on his face. At the same time he cursed himself for having been unable to prevent these senseless murders and in his heart grew a certain conviction that, unless he was able to intervene quickly, more victims would be found. He cursed himself for his helplessness, his inability to discover the motives, the methods behind the killings. It remained a mystery. Despite all his efforts, all his theorizing, his certainties and doubts, he groped in darkness. There *had* to be connection between the series of murders. But what connection? Where? Somewhere, in the disturbed brain of a man, or woman, was the key to these crimes. Who's brain? And what particular disturbance in that brain had created these bizarre killings?

Vledder came up and stood next to his old friend. The young man's face was equally serious. He gestured at the corpses.

"And I." he recriminated, "accused these people of murder." There was genuine contriteness in his voice.

DeKok glanced at him and placed a friendly hand on his shoulder.

"Don't be too upset," he counseled. "Nobody can look into the future. I, too, had not expected this."

"Drowned?" asked Vledder, sighing deeply.

DeKok rubbed the back of his neck.

"It looks that way. But more importantly, it is a clear continuation of the series. It's just that the discovery is a bit sooner than expected."

"What do you mean?"

DeKok gestured at the buckets of the dredger.

"If the dredger hadn't picked them up, they would probably not have been discovered until the end of the week, maybe later."

"So, we're close to the killer?"

"In point of time, yes."

Bram Weelen, loaded down with photographic equipment, jumped onto the deck of the dredger and looked around for a spot free of mud. Finally he placed his case inside the small steering cabin and emerged shortly thereafter with his trusty Hasselblad camera.

"Same sort of pictures?" he asked of DeKok.

"What do you suggest?" asked DeKok.

The police photographer grinned.

"Me? Nothing?" He pointed at the corpses on the deck. "I leave the suggestions to you. You just tell me what sort of pix you want and I deliver."

"Very well, Bram," answered DeKok, "deliver."

Doctor Koning carefully rolled up the cuffs of his striped pants and, supported by a helpful constable, approached. When Weelen was finished, the old Coroner knelt down next to the corpses. DeKok watched carefully and when the old man wanted to press down on Brother Rigobertus' chest, he kept the doctor's hand from descending.

"I already know," he said despondently, "that you will declare drowning as the cause of death." He paused. "I can live with that. But *this* time I want the water in the lungs to be examined in a proper laboratory."

The old Coroner looked up at the old cop.

"Are you confiscating the corpses?"

"Yes," said DeKok formally. "I'm confiscating the corpses, because I suspect foul play. Furthermore, I will insist on an autopsy." He looked defiantly around. "Nobody is going to stand in my way, this time. If necessary, I will perform the autopsy myself."

Doctor Koning did not react. Slowly he came into an upright position, helped by DeKok on one side and the constable on the other. His old bones creaked with the effort. He pointed at the corpses.

"They are dead," he declared simply.

Careful he turned around and again escorted by the constable, made his way back to the canal quay. Two morgue attendants reached down and hoisted the old man back on shore.

DeKok looked after the eccentric Coroner until he had disappeared in the back of his car. The cuffs of his striped pants were still rolled up. His large, Garibaldi hat just made it into the car before the driver slammed the door.

* * *

Young Vledder pulled up a chair and sat down.

"I personally escorted the corpses of Rigobertus and Monique to the police laboratory. They're on ice." He looked at his partner. "You're sure there's going to be an autopsy?"

DeKok smiled. There was an ironic gleam in his eyes.

"I've seldom seen our beloved Commissaris so willing and meek. For the first time in years, we parted without him yelling at me."

"We should call a press conference," grinned Vledder.

"Even the Judge-Advocate was like putty in my hands. He was actually moved to leave his ivory tower and personally consult with the Commissaris and me."

"And?"

DeKok lifted his legs to the top of his desk and leaned back with a satisfied sigh.

"Suddenly *everything* was possible. There's going to be an autopsy and an exhaustive toxicological investigation. I've been promised as much assistance as I want." He shook his head, as if answering Vledder's unspoken question. "For now I don't need any more assistance. First I have to know what sort of poison has been used. Only then will we have a change to move on. In any case . . . it's something to start with."

"You're still convinced that the victims have been poisoned?"

"Yes," nodded DeKok, "I'm convinced of that. First they were rendered helpless and then they were drowned. Nobody is going to talk me out of that. And in order to make them helpless, a substance was used." He rubbed the bridge of his nose with a little finger, then he pulled out his lower lip and let it plop back several times. Finally he rubbed the back of neck. Next he'll wiggle his eyebrows and then he's going to stare at his finger, thought Vledder. But DeKok did none of those things. "Perhaps a strong, sleep inducing substance, dissolved in a beverage," added DeKok.

"Then what?" demanded Vledder. "I mean, how did they move the unconscious corpses into Emperors Canal. Surely a person could not have done that on his, or her, own?"

DeKok suddenly looked up sharply.

"A woman!" He lifted his feet from the desk and in his typical, somewhat waddling gate, went to the coat rack.

"Rosita Stuyvenberg," he said, hoisting himself into his coat. "You remember what she said during the identification of Richard Vankerk?"

Vledder followed him on the way to the door and nodded.

"Yes," he said. "She said: *you killed him, you'll suffer for that.*"

DeKok gave him an approving look.

"Close enough. Well, Rosita Stuyvenberg has a heart full of hate and two grown sons . . . one of which has access to the temple."

"Brother Constantin of the Carillon."

"Precisely."

Vledder looked thoughtful.

"They would be . . ."

". . . ideal suspects," completed DeKok.

* * *

Again they followed the many bends of the Amstel river. The water in the river was lower this time. There was a mild, low sun in the sky and the grass along the sides of the road had gained some color. Nature seemed more friendly, more hospitable than about a week ago when they had made their way to Oldwater.

DeKok considered it a good omen. He sat up straight in his seat and looked around with interest. He came from a fishing family on the island of Urk and as such he was always a bit superstitious and that sometimes revealed itself at the most unlikely times, triggered by the most innocuous things.

The villa with the wood facade and the overhanging roof line took form as they broke through the hedge of conifers and braked on the gravel path. Slowly DeKok got out of the car. Regardless of his interest in the surroundings, a VW Beetle was just a little too small to allow his bulky frame to be transported in comfort. Vledder slammed the doors shut and together they approached the front door.

Before DeKok could touch the doorbell, the door opened.

Rosita Stuyvenberg did not seem surprised to see them. With the door in one hand and her chin in the air, she looked down at the two Inspectors, one step below her. Behind her, towering over her, they saw Brother Constantin. There was a look of tense alertness in his eyes.

DeKok lifted his hat and bowed slightly. Then he looked at mother and son.

"We're welcome . . . I hope?"

Rosita Stuyvenberg hesitated. Then she opened the door further. But her face remained even, cool and distant.

"You are welcome," she said, but the tone belied the sentiment.

She stepped back, allowed both men to precede her and closed the door behind them. Then she led the way to the spacious, high room they had visited before. She waved at some easy chairs.

The Inspectors seated themselves. Rosita and her son sat down across from them. Vledder watched them carefully. Their attitude, their demeanor, was uncertain, tense, as if they were ill at ease. Rosita sat up straight, her oval face was pale and Brother Constantin seemed to have lost some of his self-possession.

DeKok searched for an opening and coughed discreetly.

"We came to bring you greetings from Brother Rigobertus," he said in a sepulchral tone of voice.

Rosita Stuyvenberg reacted sharply. Her eyes flickered.

"That is . . . is distasteful, Inspector," she said. "Brother Rigobertus is dead and you know it." She looked at her son. "Alfred saw both of you, yesterday, on the dredger."

DeKok looked her in the eyes. There was amazement in his own eyes.

"Alfred . . . or should I say, Brother Constantin, apparently has the admirable gift of being always in the right place at the right time." His voice dripped with sarcasm. "If I remember correctly, he was also a witness at the time that your husband and that . . . girl were fished out of the waters of Emperors Canal."

Brother Constantin gave him a castigating look.

"Your sarcasm is misplaced," he censured. "Both times I happened to have just left our premises at Emperors Canal. It was pure coincidence. And, I assure you, not a pleasant experience at all. No matter what Richard was during his lifetime, he *was* my father." He bent his head in sadness. "Brother Rigobertus, our leader, was always very much admired by me."

DeKok rubbed the bridge of his nose with a little finger. Then he held it up in the air and stared at it for several long seconds, as if he had never seen it before. Still contemplating his finger, he asked casually:

"Are you ready to take his place?"

The polished expression on Brother Constantin's face suddenly changed. He was obviously beginning to get agitated. His face flushed, red spots appeared on his cheeks. For a fleeting moment DeKok thought about the Commissaris and his rages.

159

Then he paid careful attention to the words spoken by Constantin.

"Brother Crispin and I will have to consult on that."

"What about Brother Cornelis?"

A pitying smile played around the other's lips.

"Brother Cornelis only has interest in his voices."

"And you?"

"The preservation of our Community is at stake. That is certain. We must take action, soon, in order to . . ."

". . . to stop the serial killings?" interrupted DeKok.

Brother Constantin jumped out of his chair as if bitten by a snake.

"Our Community has nothing to do with the murders," he exclaimed vehemently.

DeKok feigned surprise. He fell back in his chair and looked up at the excited man.

"Well, that *does* surprise me," DeKok said in a bemused tone of voice. "But," he continued, pointedly, "isn't it remarkable that all the older members of the Carillon and the beloved leader, Rigobertus, have been systematically removed . . ." He paused and smiled sweetly, ". . . to make room for the younger generation, perhaps?"

Brother Constantin reacted angrily. He leaned forward and seemed to tower over DeKok. There was hate and the promise of violence in his eyes.

"That's a lie!" he shouted. "A scurrilous accusation!"

Rosita stood up as well. She took her son by the arm and pulled him back.

"Alfred," she said sternly, "control yourself."

Brother Constantin sank back in his chair. Mrs. Stuyvenberg remained standing. She turned toward DeKok, cool, almost regal.

"Your theories regarding these murders," she said icily, "do not interest us in the least. When you think you have enough evidence against us, against any of us, you may return to discharge your official duties. Until that time we wish to be spared your intrusions into our privacy." She took a deep breath. "I find your behavior reprehensible. The way you confronted me with that . . . eh, that Miss Vankerk at the morgue was less than tactful."

DeKok bowed his head in shame.

"You are right. My profession sometimes forces me to act unfriendly, or less than tactful than is normally to be expected." He stood up and gave her his winningest smile. "Please accept my sincere apologies." He motioned toward Vledder. "We will no longer abuse your hospitality."

Just as he was ready to leave the room, his attention was drawn to a photograph in a silver frame on the oak sideboard. It was the portrait of a young man and a young woman.

Rosita Stuyvenberg stood next to him.

"My son Adrian and Jessica," she said.

DeKok caught his breath. The photograph seemed to keep him spellbound.

"Who's Jessica?"

The woman next to him hesitated. He heard her breathing.

"Jessica is . . . was Adrian's fiance. She died tragically."

DeKok studied the photo carefully. He was just about to replace the silver frame when a young man entered the room. Suddenly, without warning, he stormed toward DeKok and ripped the photograph out of his hands. He looked at Rosita, a furious look on his face.

"How many times have I told you that I don't want this photo displayed?"

With quick, angry steps he left the room, carrying the framed photo with him.

Rosita Stuyvenberg shook her head sadly.

"Adrian . . . he hasn't been the same since her death."

15

When Vledder entered the detective room, DeKok looked up from his papers and waved for him across the room. Vledder approached and sank down on a chair.

"How was the autopsy?" asked DeKok.

"Dr. Rusteloos was very fast," smiled Vledder. "He put everything else aside and he was finished in less than three hours."

"Both of them?"

Vledder nodded.

"I've never seen him, and his assistant, work that fast. It was a madhouse. They had at least four other autopsies scheduled."

"Anything particular at this time?"

"Brother Rigobertus had an enlarged liver and Monique may have been troubled by kidney stones."

"Cause of death?"

"What do you think?"

"Drowning?"

Vledder made a helpless gesture.

"I told Dr. Rusteloos about the previous cases. I also told him about your suspicions and . . . he agreed. But for now he could not, in all conscience, come to a different conclusion."

DeKok rubbed the back of his neck.

"Let's hope that the toxicological inquiry will give us better results. Did you, personally, escort the samples to Dr. Eskes?"

"Of course," said Vledder. "You had asked me specifically. I told him you were in a hurry and he told me that was nothing new. He did ask if you were looking for a specific poison."

DeKok shook his head.

"I daren't suggest anything in that area. I simply don't know. There are so many possibilities ... as long as it isn't immediately fatal."

They both remained silent for a long time. Finally, as usual, Vledder broke the silence.

"What have you been doing, in the mean time?"

"I," smiled DeKok, "Have been busy with a family drama."

"What family ... and what drama?"

DeKok tapped the papers on his desk.

"Mother Stuyvenberg, her son Adrian ... and the tragic death of Jessica."

"The girl in the photo?"

"Jessica Wineguard. She committed suicide."

"Suicide?"

DeKok waved at the papers on his desk.

"I read the reports that were made as a result of the investigation in the death. It's a strange case."

"Any indications of criminal intent?"

"Not exactly." DeKok shook his head. "It was clearly suicide. The thing is, however, that there was no apparent reason for it."

"In other words," said Vledder, "you mean that on the surface there was no reason for her to want to kill herself?"

"Precisely."

"How did she kill herself?"

"She hanged herself."

* * *

DeKok studied the woman in front of him. He estimated her to be in her late forties. She had an almost round face with slightly protruding, high cheekbones. The skin was smooth and glowing. The wavy, silver-gray hair was kept in check with a nearly unnoticeable net.

"Mrs. Wineguard?" he asked amicably.

She looked at the two men on her doorstep. There was a hint of surprise and suspicion in her blue eyes.

"Yes . . . yes, that's me," she admitted hesitantly.

The gray sleuth smiled.

"My name is DeKok . . . with . . . eh, with kay-oh-kay." He pointed at Vledder. "My colleague, Vledder. We're from the police."

"Inspectors?"

"Just so. We wanted to talk to you about the death of your daughter, Jessica."

She stepped back and allowed the men to enter. Through a nicely decorated foyer with an intricately carved chest, they reached a tastefully furnished living room. On the mantel piece DeKok discovered a duplicate of the photo and silver frame he had seen in the Stuyvenberg residence.

DeKok looked around and then sat down on a carved bench. He pointed at the mantel piece.

"A handsome couple. Those two must have loved each other dearly."

"That is right," she said, as she seated herself on a chair across from DeKok. "Adrian is a dear boy. He was, still is, inconsolable."

"And you?"

She adjusted a sleeve of her dress.

"I have learned to live with it. My husband died a year earlier. Sorrow cleanses one."

DeKok nodded sympathetically.

"Did you have a good relationship with your daughter?"

"Certainly. We've always been a rather close family. Happily so. Jessica loved her father very much, more than she loved me. But after my husband died, we grew closer together. She confided more in me."

DeKok bit his lips, weighing his next question.

"But her death was unexpected, surely? I mean, there was nothing before that could have hinted at suicide?"

She shook her head slowly.

"I've thought about it and thought about it. I just cannot conceive of what the problem might have been. Everything seemed fine . . . no problems of any kind."

"She never discussed any difficulties with you?"

"Why should she?" Mrs. Wineguard sounded just a bit irritated. "There were no problems as far as I knew. On the contrary. Jessica was very happy. She and Adrian had just become engaged and it was quite a party. They looked forward to getting married and were looking for a house."

"In the reports it was mentioned that she did not want to receive Adrian the night before she died. She locked herself in her room and was not seen again."

"That's correct."

"But something must have happened?" pressed DeKok.

Mrs. Wineguard shook her head, a sad look on her face.

"I wouldn't know what. Jessica was a dear and intelligent child. She was universally liked, was very dedicated and had just been installed."

DeKok moved in his chair.

"Installed?"

"Yes," nodded the mother, "She was, as were my husband and I, a member of the Community of the Brothers and Sisters of the Holy Blessings."

DeKok swallowed.

"Installed?" repeated DeKok.

"She had been installed as the first female member of the Carillon."

DeKok groaned softly and looked at the ceiling. Slowly his gaze lowered until he stared at Mrs. Wineguard with an unbelieving look on his face.

"Sister Charisse."

* * *

They drove back to Warmoes Street in silence. It was already dark and a drizzly rain clung to the windows of the car. Harsh neon advertisements mirrored in the wet asphalt. DeKok was relaxed, hands on his knees. The monotonous movement of the window wipers had a sophomoric effect on him. He felt he was close to the solution. The photos had provided him with a golden thread. There had to be a connection between Jessica's death and the following murders. There was no other way. As soon as he discovered the few missing links, he would be able to forge an unbreakable chain of events . . . a chain of events that would lead to the perpetrator, or perpetrators. That was his task. He smiled. How much incriminating evidence had he gathered over the years? He decided not to worry about it.

Vledder, at the wheel, stared somberly at the road. Every once in a while he would quickly glance aside. There was a particular expression on the face of his old partner . . . a look he had learned to recognize over the years. He knew that DeKok was close to a solution, had an instinctive feeling about the how and why of the killings. It irked him that he, although aware of the same facts as his partner, was still groping in the dark. But he was just a little too proud and, let's face it, too pig-headed, he admitted to himself, to ask for clarification.

There happened to be a parking spot in front of the station and it was unoccupied. Vledder drove the car into the slot and switched off the engine. As they passed the counter that separated the public part of the station from the rest, the Watch Commander yelled at them.

DeKok recognized the unmistakable voice of Meindert Post and ambled over. Post handed him a letter.

"For you," he growled.

DeKok looked at the envelope. There was no stamp, no postmark, no sender. He looked up.

"How did you get it?"

Meindert Post shrugged massive shoulders.

"Must have been delivered. Suddenly it was on the counter. You know how it is, around here. Busier than Central Station. I saw your name and was going to send it up to the detective room, but they said you'd gone out. I figured you'd pass here sooner or later . . . you, or your side-kick there." He grinned at Vledder.

DeKok ripped open the envelope and took out the contents.

It was a short note:

"*Dear Sir:*

"*You should take a look in the studio of the sculptor Zanderveen on Prince's Island. You will be amazed.*"

The letter was written in peculiar, slanted block letters. There was no signature, no date. He handed the letter to Vledder. After he had also read it, he looked at DeKok.

"Sculptor Zanderveen . . . a well-known artist. He creates some fine pieces. Usually in bronze. I've seen the studio. An impressive man." He shook his head. "What do we want with a sculptor?"

168

DeKok took back the letter and put it nonchalantly in one of the pockets of his raincoat. Then he turned around and headed for the exit at a fast trot.

Vledder paused a moment to enjoy the view. DeKok at speed was a comical sight.

"Where are you going?" called Vledder.

DeKok stopped at the door and turned around.

"To Prince's Island . . . to be amazed."

* * *

From Harlem Square they drove under the viaduct toward the New Tar Gardens, rattled across the old cantilever bridge and turned into Gallows Street.

Vledder gestured toward the windshield.

"It's to the left on Prince's Island, not too far from the chicken bridge. Zanderveen lives close to his studio in a small house. They say that it used to be the studio of Breitner."

"I've often wondered what happens to all those studios. Rembrandt's, of course, has become a museum and so have a number of others. The rest, I suppose get recycled, so to speak."

"That's right, although Breitner's studio should probably also have become a museum."

"Why? Was he *that* famous? I knew he was well-known as a painter of Amsterdam city-scapes, but what else did he do?"

"He moved to Amsterdam from The Hague in 1886 and then became one of the leading figures in the so-called 'Eighties Movement,' that's 1880, not 1980. He was considered one of the foremost Dutch impressionists until about 1894 when he started to concentrate more and more on photography. He was also one of the first to use photographs as an aid to creating his paintings. He was not really appreciated until the late 1920s and his paintings are now worth millions."

"Refresh me on the Eighties Movement," said DeKok, "I always forget that you have a degree in history."

"The Eighties Movement," answered Vledder, "was basically a group of leading painters, authors and poets of the time. They were headquartered in Amsterdam. One of their best known members was Willem Kloos, the poet, who proposed universal suffrage as early as 1891. And I mean *universal* suffrage: men, women, rich and poor, property owners and bums. It made the movement less than popular with the powers that be." He grinned at DeKok. "It would have been the type of organization you would have felt comfortable in," he added.

"I don't like organizations," protested DeKok.

"Well, that gives you some idea about Breitner and his time. He died poor, of course, just like Van Gogh who, incidentally, painted his 'Potato Eaters' in 1885 and who died in 1891."

"Ah, thanks, that helps to place it in context."

Vledder was used to DeKok's non-sequiturs and meanderings into subjects that were not really a part of the case. But now he felt the time had come to get back to the subject at hand.

"Do you have any idea where the letter may have come from?" asked Vledder.

"No," said DeKok, taking the letter out of his coat pocket. "But I should perhaps be a little more careful with it. I may need it to compare handwritings."

"All right, but where did it come from?"

DeKok shrugged as if the subject was unimportant.

"The letter itself surprises me more than its origin."

"Why?"

"It's the first time during this case that someone has contacted me with a hint." DeKok grimaced. "If we don't count Little Lowee. Anyway," he continued, "I'm looking forward to whatever we may find in the studio."

Vledder parked the VW next to a wooden fence and they got out. Prince's Island, an almost square parcel of two city blocks, hemmed in by warehouses and four different canals, was badly lit. There were many dark corners and the facades of the old warehouses, many converted to lofts, rose around them like threatening guardians from a time long ago. The entire area breathed an atmosphere of secretiveness.

Vledder rang the bell of the small house with the peeled door. It took some time and then a big, bearded man appeared in the door opening. A black sweater strained against the contours of a large chest and impressive shoulders.

DeKok rubbed the back of his neck. The term "barrel-chested" came immediately to mind when seeing the man.

"We're Police Inspectors," DeKok introduced them. "Attached to Warmoes Street station. An anonymous letter directed us to your studio. I know it sounds strange, but we would like to take a look around your studio."

The man was taken aback.

"At this hour?"

"You would oblige us very much," answered DeKok. "It's part of an investigation into a series of double murders. Something, or someone, in your studio might give us a lead." He gestured apologetically. "At least, I hope so."

The sculptor shook his head.

"I don't know anything about murders," he rumbled. "But . . . if you want to look around . . . be my guest." He went inside and returned shortly, wearing a rain slicker. "It's close by, follow me."

The three of them walked across the worn cobble stones. Their footsteps echoed against the surrounding buildings with a hollow sound.

They reached the studio and the sculptor opened a padlock and pushed the large door aside. Then he disappeared in the dark.

171

Suddenly the interior was bathed in strong lights. The two cops stared into a large, messy space. Everything was covered in a thin layer of gray-white dust. A tall, striking sculpture group stood in the center of the space. Slowly they picked their way further into the studio and looked up at the sculpture.

The group consisted of a man and a woman. They stood next to each other, heads raised, arms entwined and fingers entangled in a complicated grip.

Vledder's mouth fell open.

"The victims," he spluttered.

DeKok stared up at the sculpture with amazement.

"The way there were fished out of the canal."

16

Sculptor Zanderveen muttered in his beard.

"Don't read newspapers," he said, "haven't for years. Nothing but bad news, anyway . . . murder, mayhem, politics. They go well together: politics, murder and intrigue. Don't want nothing to do with it all."

"But you live in the world, you're part of it."

"Says you."

DeKok smiled. He was not in the mood for a discussion of politics. Quickly he went back to the subject of his investigation.

"So, you had never heard about the double murders?"

"No, told you."

DeKok pointed at the sculpture.

"Why did you decide on that sculpture?"

Zanderveen shrugged his broad shoulders.

"It's a commission."

"From whom?"

"Don't know."

"But's that's strange," said DeKok amazement in his voice and on his face. "Somebody must have told you what was wanted."

"Sure," said Zanderveen, nodding slowly. "Got a detailed letter . . . and a photo." He gestured with his right hand. Not the whole picture, just a part, a fragment. Two arms entwined, fingers interlaced. Had to become a group ... a man and a woman, holding each other like that."

"Nothing else? No indication about age, expression, likeness ... that sort of thing?"

Zanderveen did not seem to care.

"Had to be somebody's impression of love ... a look into the future."

"Do you still have the fragment of the photo?"

"No." Zanderveen shook his head. "Once I knew what they wanted, I threw it away."

"What about the letter?"

"That too."

DeKok swallowed, completely taken aback.

"But you don't just begin a sculpture of that size on the basis of an anonymous letter?"

"Why not?"

DeKok grinned, still bemused.

"But somebody has to pay for it, surely?"

Zanderveen nodded emphatically.

"Sure. There was money with the letter. One hundred thousand guilders. Exactly one hundred notes of a thousand each."

* * *

They drove away from the studio on Prince's Island. DeKok was sprawled low in his seat, a contented look on his face. The jig-saw puzzle started to fit together ... a picture of hate and passion emerged. Absent-mindedly he began to search his pockets for a forgotten piece of candy. Vledder interrupted the search and his musings.

"The money for the sculpture," exclaimed the young man, "that must have been part of the money Richard Vankerk took out of the bank that day."

DeKok nodded slowly.

"The murderer found a use for it."

"A strange use . . . if you ask me."

DeKok hoisted himself in a more upright position.

"Not really. He knew exactly what he was doing. The sculpture is a symbol of the murders."

Vledder snorted.

"Love and a look toward the future. Nice future . . . death by drowning."

DeKok pushed his hat further back on his head.

"I don't think you should look at it that way." He paused, looked out of the window, then at Vledder. "Do you have any guesses about from what photograph came the fragment that was sent to the sculptor?"

Vledder did not answer at once. His attention was on a tricky intersection. Suddenly his face lit up.

"The photo from the silver frame. That's it! You're right. In the picture those two had about the same pose . . . Adrian and Jessica." Suddenly a haunted look came into his eyes. His mouth fell open. Involuntarily he turned toward DeKok. "But . . . but that means that . . . Adrian is . . ."

DeKok pointed through the windshield.

"I'd stop here, if I were you. This is the station."

* * *

They passed the counter. Meindert Post had meanwhile been relieved. The current Watch Commander waved heartily as they went by. DeKok waved back. Then, with two, three treads at a time, he climbed the stairs to the next floor. There was an unnatural calm in the large detective room. Only Inspector Prins was seated behind a desk, typing a report. As Vledder and DeKok entered, he looked up.

"Any news," he asked, interested.

DeKok grinned.

"More or less. We only have to find the perpetrator."

Fred Prins laughed.

"Isn't that the story of our life," he joked. "Police work would be easy, if it wasn't for all the crime." He pointed at his desk. "Have you seen the Commissaris yet?"

DeKok was surprised.

"No, why should I?"

"Because he's been waiting for you."

"He's in the station? At this hour?"

"Sure is."

"What does he want?"

Prins shrugged his shoulders.

"I don't know, I'd be the last to know. But he did say that he wanted to see you as soon as you came in."

* * *

DeKok knocked, a bit diffidently. It was highly unusual for the Commissaris to be in the station at such a late hour. He was strictly a nine-to-five man. When DeKok heard a noise from the other side of the door, he took it as an invitation and stepped into the commissarial office.

Commissaris Buitendam immediately came from behind his desk and walked toward DeKok with outstretched hands. He placed an arm around DeKok's shoulder and led him to a chair in front of his desk.

176

DeKok looked suspicious. In DeKok's mind, chiefs had their place and he did not, in principle object to them. But they should not meddle in what DeKok considered to be *his* business.

The Commissaris sat back behind his desk and cleared his throat.

"I stayed over, tonight," he began in his cultivated, somewhat affected voice. "Or rather, I came back after dinner, because I thought it was important . . . that is, I felt I should personally inform you."

"What?" DeKok was curious.

Buitendam hesitated visibly.

"I . . . eh, I received the preliminary toxicological report from Dr. Eskes."

"And?"

The Commissaris sighed deeply.

"There were no noticeable traces of poison in the bodies of . . . eh . . ." He consulted his notes. "Oh, yes . . . in the bodies of Brother Rigobertus and Monique Vankerk."

Abruptly DeKok leaned forward.

"No poison!" he exclaimed, upset.

Commissaris Buitendam shook his head.

"I asked for further details by telephone and Dr. Eskes told me that he tested for most of the more common poisons. Without results. Of course, it is possible, according to Dr. Eskes that a heretofore unknown poison has been used, but although possible, it was not considered probable."

DeKok sank back in his chair. His face was serious. The result of the toxicological investigation had, to say the least, taken him by surprise. He had been sure that poison had been used.

"What now, DeKok?"

"I must admit," answered DeKok, "that a negative report never entered my mind."

The Commissaris came to his feet.

"I also talked to the Judge-Advocate. Nevertheless he expects results."

DeKok also stood up. He felt the anger building up and knew that his cheeks were getting red. The inconsistent attitude of the powers that be made him furious. Until recently he had experienced nothing but negativism and obstructionism. If they only had allowed an autopsy in the very beginning, then . . . It was as if something in his brain suddenly snapped. His train of thought was roughly interrupted. The victims were helpless before they were drowned. Did that necessarily mean a poison? He looked at the Commissaris, who looked at him as if he had seen a ghost. He shrugged the Commissaris to the background of his thinking. There were other possibilities. Gas! Abruptly he turned around and walked out of the office.

The Commissaris called after him, but DeKok did not hear it.

* * *

Back in the detective room, DeKok addressed Inspector Prins.

"Are you available?"

"What for?"

"To come with Vledder and me."

Prins was already on his feet.

"Sure . . . is there going to be an arrest?"

DeKok did not answer. He pointed at a row of car keys.

"Take a car that will run and follow us."

"Where are we going?"

"Emperors Canal."

Vledder looked at DeKok with a look of total incomprehension.

"Whatever for?" asked Vledder.

DeKok smiled.

"Breaking and entering . . . in the house of the Brothers and Sisters of the Holy Blessings."

Prins' face fell.

"Breaking *and* entering?"

DeKok looked at his watch and nodded.

"It's a good time for it."

Prins made a helpless gesture.

"What can I do . . . I mean, breaking and entering. Are you serious?"

"Sure," grinned DeKok. "As for what you can do . . . ever heard of a look-out?"

* * *

Emperors Canal was deserted. The water shimmered from a few streetlights and far away was the dull sound of traffic crossing Town Hall Street. A sole rat scurried between the parked cars. The buildings were dark.

DeKok stopped in front of the house belonging to the Community of Brothers and Sisters and looked up. It was a normal canal house, a half-sunken basement and bluestone steps leading up to the front door. There was a different doorbell for each floor. He looked at the basement doors, but dismissed them . . . they were usually closed with a wooden, or steel beam from the inside.

Carefully he climbed the steps toward the front door. He stood still on the porch. He looked around. Some distance away, in the shadow of a tree, he saw Vledder. On the other side, almost at the corner of Gentlemen Street, he could just see the outline of Prins. He chuckled to himself. If something went wrong, the powers that be would have some explaining to do.

Suddenly he realized that there were no cars parked along the water in front of this particular building. A white square had been painted on the cobblestone and instead of the universal sign for "Handicapped", the word had been painted in the center of the square with big block letters. It was different from regular handicapped spaces, which were in any case usually indicated by a sign on a pole. There was something about the lettering that struck him as familiar.

He turned around and pulled a small instrument from his pocket. It was an innocuous looking copper tube. The gift from Handy Henkie, a notorious burglar. When Henkie decided to go straight, he gave his "magic door opener", as he called it, to DeKok. The small instrument had never yet failed DeKok. Henkie was now gainfully employed as an instrument maker and it was ironic that he made more money in his respectable profession than he had ever done as a burglar.

It took DeKok exactly eighty seconds to open the door and nobody would later be able to prove that the lock had been forced. He pushed against the heavy door and when he did not hear an alarm, he walked back to the railing of the porch and motioned toward Vledder and Prins. They immediately joined him and the three of them entered the premises. DeKok carefully closed the now unlocked door behind them.

The light of Vledder's flashlight made bizarre ovals on the walls and ceiling of the corridor.

"What do we do if somebody suddenly shows up?" asked Prins in a whisper. Fred Prins had never been this close to one of DeKok's illegal entries.

DeKok grinned.

"Then we tell them that, much to our shock and surprise, we found the front door unlocked. And because we suspected foul play, we decided to investigate."

"And they'll believe that?"

"Often, my boy, quite often."

Vledder nudged him in the back.

"I don't understand what you're looking for, DeKok. What do you think you'll find?"

"I don't know exactly what it will look like," evaded DeKok. "I have only the vaguest image in my mind."

Stairs at the end of the long corridor led downward. Carefully they descended. The old, wooden steps creaked under their feet.

The ceiling in the basement floor was low. In a crouch they walked toward the front of the building. Suddenly DeKok stopped dead in his tracks. The light of his flashlight played across a low cart with bicycle wheels. It was not much of a cart. Just a wide shelf on an axle between two wheels. DeKok stroked the wood with his hand. It was still damp.

Vledder leaned over him.

"What's that?"

"And now we commit their bodies to the deep . . ."

"What!?"

DeKok stared somberly into a dark corner of the basement.

"The contraption for launching."

17

Inspector DeKok put Handy Henkie's invention back in his pocket. The door of the old canal house had been closed exactly as they had found it. The two younger Inspectors waited at the bottom of the bluestone steps. DeKok walked down to join them.

Vledder gestured toward the basement floor.

"Shouldn't we have confiscated that cart?"

"Later."

"What if the murderer makes it disappear?"

DeKok pursed his lips and shook his head.

"He won't get the chance," said DeKok nonchalantly.

He ambled down the side of the canal into the direction of the old Beetle. Vledder and Prins followed.

Now that the end was near, DeKok felt strange, unfulfilled and almost uncomfortable. He knew the killer and his motives. If he followed his preference, he would now just as soon go home and leave the case to others. But that was impossible. He was a Police Inspector, a civil servant, specifically hired to solve crimes and to deliver the perpetrators to justice. That was his task. He waited when he reached the cars. Prins' car was parked right behind the old VW.

When Prins and Vledder reached him they noticed his indecisiveness. For a long time the three just stood there, looking at each other. Vledder, who had known DeKok longer, understood some of what bothered the older man.

"What . . . eh, what now?" he asked softly.

DeKok lowered his head and bit his lower lip. For another second or two he seemed to hesitate. Then he lifted his head.

"Back to Round Hoop," he said hoarsely, "in Oldwater on the Amstel . . . you can ride with us, Fred."

* * *

Again they followed the bends, twists and turns of the Amstel river. DeKok ignored the pale moon that forged a silver path on the rippling water. His thoughts were occupied by the upcoming confrontation. The countryside was asleep and theirs was the only vehicle that moved. When they arrived at the villa, they slowed down and the headlights illuminated the fine, wooden facade of the structure. The Inspectors stepped out of the car and with DeKok in the middle, they approached the front door of the house.

Probably alerted by the noise of the car on the gravel driveway and the sweep of the headlights, Rosita Stuyvenberg opened the door herself and stepped outside. Calmly she looked at the tense faces of the cops. The night air was chilly and she crossed her arms, as if to warm herself. An involuntary shiver ran down her spine. But there was a dark, dangerous glow in her eyes. She pulled her head slightly back, looking down her nose at the unwelcome visitors.

"An ungodly hour," she said sharply.

"One cannot always choose the hour," answered DeKok resignedly.

She gave him an arrogant, denigrating look.

"What are you doing here?"

DeKok did not answer at once. For several seconds he looked her in the eyes.

"We come to take away yours sons," he said finally, tonelessly. "And," he added, "the key to the temple in Duivendrecht."

The two sons emerged from the darkness beyond the front door and stood next to their mother. The confrontation had something threatening about it. Then Alfred Vankerk took a half step forward.

"We heard, Mother. Let us go. It will soon be clear that we're innocent."

DeKok looked at him.

"This is not an arrest, Brother Constantin."

Rosita Stuyvenberg's eyes narrowed.

"No arrest?" she asked, suspicion in her voice.

DeKok shook his head.

"No, no, not at all ... just a friendly request for cooperation." He looked at Adrian. "And I expect that nobody will object to *that*."

* * *

The gray brick wall around the temple looked even more uninviting and inhospitable in the dark of night and the glass shards and broken bottles on the top were clearly visible in the half light of the moon. They walked across the coarse gravel toward the cast-iron gate. Brother Constantin pulled out a security card and inserted it in the slot. Almost soundlessly, the doors opened. With a regular key Brother Constantin opened the door under the gothic archway.

It was almost dark in the hall, moonlight barely penetrated through the glass-in-lead windows. Carefully they walked from the hall to the temple. It was even darker there. Brother

Constantin and Adrian led the way. The three Inspectors followed close behind.

Suddenly the entire space was bathed in harsh light. DeKok looked around. Apart from his group, there was nobody else in sight. He noticed that the red velvet cushions in the center had been rearranged. They now formed a square. The light was reflected from the open baptismal basin. They halted on the place for the choir. Five men in a rough circle, nervously, almost anxiously looking around.

DeKok realized full well that there was danger . . . deadly danger. But he had no idea from which direction it would manifest itself. Sharply, intensely, he listened for the least sound. He suspected that all the victims had stood thus, before they had lost consciousness and had been pushed into the basin.

Suddenly a sound came nearer. It came from all sides. Overpowering, penetrating. A large, mighty choir reached a crescendo. "Nearer my God to Thee," descended upon them.

DeKok suddenly moved. His movement was so quick that Vledder did not realize the old man had moved until DeKok was already several steps away. DeKok ran across the lush carpets to a side door of the temple. Adrian was the first one to follow him.

DeKok pulled open the door. The room beyond, full of technical apparatus, was occupied by a single man in a long, gray duster. The man staggered, brought his hands up to his throat and then fell to the ground with a dull thud.

Adrian knelt down next to him. He took the man's head in his arms. With shaking hands he cradled it against his chest.

"Brother Cornelis," he sobbed, "you mustn't die."

18

Inspector DeKok opened the door of his house. Vledder stood outside, a shy smile on his face and a large bouquet of roses in his hands.

"Fred here yet?"

DeKok helped the young man out of his coat and nodded.

"He's in the living room, with my wife. As usual, he's talking up a storm."

"What about?

DeKok grinned mockingly.

"About the many crimes he has solved during his career."

Vledder rubbed the bridge of his nose with a little finger.

"He's still a rookie."

Together they entered the living room. Mrs. DeKok immediately stood up and greeted Vledder heartily. She managed a charming little blush when Vledder handed her the roses.

DeKok reached for a bottle of fine cognac and carefully poured into the pre-warmed glasses. Fred Prins gestured toward the old man, as he addressed Vledder.

"He didn't want to say a thing until you were here."

Vledder winked at DeKok as he accepted his glass. He cradled the glass between his fingers and rocked it slightly, watching the amber liquid cling briefly to the sides of the paper-thin snifter. Then he brought the glass close to his nose and inhaled the aroma with sensuous pleasure.

Fred Prins looked on in amazement. Vledder was getting to be a connoisseur of cognac, he thought, it must be DeKok's influence. It was well known that cognac was DeKok's favorite beverage and that he held reverent views about the double-distilled wine.

Vledder took a careful sip and placed the glass on a convenient side table.

"Before I came here," said DeKok's younger partner, "I stopped by at the Wilhelmina Hospital. Apparently Brother Cornelis is going to pull through. The duty doctor was very optimistic. They were able to neutralize the poison he had taken."

DeKok nodded as he made his way to his favorite chair. He sat down and took a sip from the glass in his hand. He looked over the rim of his glass at Prins.

"Come on, Fred, try it, you'll like it." Then, as Prins took his first, careful sip, DeKok turned toward Vledder.

"I saw him this afternoon, Brother Cornelis, I mean. The doctors allowed me a brief visit. There were a few points that needed clearing up."

"Did he confess?"

"Completely. He had intended to commit suicide. But I think that, in retrospect, he was glad we prevented that."

Mrs. DeKok entered with a large tray, covered with several platters of various delicacies. Fred Prins put down his glass and hastened to help her place the tray on the sideboard. She thanked him with a smile.

"If they keep him alive," she wanted to know, "what sort of punishment will they give a man like that?"

DeKok made a vague gesture.

"It depends on what the psychiatrists have to say about it. If he's declared mentally incompetent, he'll be classified as 'at the disposition of the government' and that means confinement in a psychiatric institution for an undetermined time."

Mrs. DeKok handed her husband one of the platters.

"Do you have any doubt?" she asked.

"About his mental capacities?"

"Yes."

DeKok shook his head and took another sip from his cognac. He passed the platter on to Prins, who handed it to Vledder, after he made a selection.

"Well?" urged DeKok's wife.

"Brother Cornelis has a good brain," said DeKok slowly. "I mean, he's intelligent. He was a formidable opponent." He paused and put his glass down and leaned back in his chair. "No matter how much experience a cop has, I don't think it's possible to have an error-free investigation. This time, too, I made a number of mistakes."

That was too much for Prins.

"You, DeKok, mistakes? Come, now ..."

The gray sleuth nodded seriously, a painful look on his face.

"When the first corpses where fished from the canal, I assumed, hear me, *assumed* that the water Dr. Koning pressed out of the lungs, had to be canal water. If I had been more alert at the time, I could have *proved*, even without an autopsy, that the victims had not drowned in the canal ... but had been dumped into the canal *after* they had drowned."

Vledder shook his head.

"Tap water, containing chlorine and the usual purifiers, from the baptismal basin. It would have been easy to check that, especially in a lab."

DeKok shrugged sheepishly.

"My second mistake was that I paid too much attention to the happenings in Cortina d'Ampezzo. There were so many obvious motives, that the true reason for the murders was completely overlooked."

Vledder protested.

"I don't agree with you. All the leads pointed to the meeting in Cortina. We had no other choice. It would have been irresponsible if we had ignored it. It was only *after* we found Brother Rigobertus and Monique in the canal that we could even *suspect* that the meeting in Cortina had nothing to do with the true motives of the case."

DeKok gave Vledder an appreciative look.

"Thanks for the defense," he said, "but I still think it was incomplete. I should, from the very start, have paid more attention to the symbolism."

Prins looked a question.

"What symbolism?

DeKok sighed.

"The corpses were always found in the same position. Arms entwined, fingers laced together. The perpetrator wanted to express something. Well, that is the symbolism I did not understand."

Vledder was irritated.

"But was it possible to understand the symbolism? I tried, but there was no sane conclusion to be drawn."

DeKok took another sip and thoughtfully selected a tidbit from the platter next to him. He chewed pensively and took another sip. Then he said:

"It's always difficult to imagine yourself in the position of the murderer. Especially if one is not familiar with the background, it becomes almost impossible to think like he does. The entwined arms, the locked fingers . . . it could have been a symbol for love . . . for young love. But the male victims were all

190

well past fifty. Some men can still be passionate at that age, but ..." He did not finish the sentence. He cocked his head. "I felt I was looking in the wrong direction. The symbolism did not apply to the victims."

"Where did it apply," Prins wanted to know.

"It may sound strange, but I found my first, *real* clue when I saw the photo in the silver frame, the one at Rosita Stuyvenberg's house. Two young people in love, who held on to each other in the same way as we had found with the corpses. It could, of course, have been mere coincidence ... but somehow I was convinced that there was more to it than that."

Vledder made an impatient gesture.

"Then why did Adrian pull the photo from your hands?"

"Adrian," answered DeKok solemnly, "knew from the very beginning who the killer was."

"Did he say so?"

"No," said DeKok. "But then ... I didn't ask him to tell me."

Mrs. DeKok moved closer to the edge of her chair.

"Then what," she asked, "does Adrian have to do with the murders?"

"Nothing ... and everything."

Mrs. DeKok was less than pleased.

"That's no answer," she said sternly.

"Sorry, my dear," answered her husband. "I was coming to that. You see," he continued, "Adrian was engaged to be married to Jessica. They were both very much in love. They made an ideal couple and they were full of hope for the future. Both had, since childhood, been members of the Community of the Brothers and Sisters of the Holy Blessings and were well regarded within the community. When there was a vacancy in the Carillon, Jessica was chosen and installed as Sister Charisse. Charisse means 'comely'. The man who proposed the name and who had worked hard to have her win the nomination was . . . her uncle, Brother Cornelis."

"Her uncle?"

"Yes," nodded DeKok. "The only brother of Jessica's late father. You see, Brother Cornelis' family name was Wineguard. Brother Cornelis never married. His entire life was devoted to the Community. He is an honest and sincerely devout human being and he observed with sorrow the way the leaders of the Community behaved immorally, perverted the very concept of the Community. Because he wanted to avoid a schism within the community, he remained silent. But, inevitably, some of the excesses and scandals leaked out. Originally Cornelis planned to change the membership of the Carillon gradually. He planned to replace the old guard, so to speak, consisting of the likes of Brother Castor and Brother Christian with new, more sincere individuals. He felt that women would be more suitable to lead the Community onto moral paths. His nomination of Jessica was the first step in his long-range plan."

DeKok lowered his head and fell silent. He contemplated his empty glass and looked around for the bottle. Mrs. DeKok handed it to him. As he poured, he thought again about the deathly pale man in the white hospital bed. He felt a wave of pity for Brother Cornelis.

Fred Prins felt no pity, just eagerness to know more.

"Well," he said. "What happened next?"

DeKok looked up.

"Brothers Rigobertus, Christian and Castor invited Sister Charisse for her first meeting of the Carillon. The meeting was to be held in the office of Brother Rigobertus. Before the meeting the men had consumed a considerable amount of alcohol. When Sister Charisse, Jessica, entered she was immediately aware of the condition the men were in. She announced that she would leave and return when they were sober. The men became angry.

192

There was a short exchange of words, then they overpowered her and raped her."

"All three of them?"

His audience was stunned. Rape is almost unheard of in Holland and is severely punished on the rare occasions when it does happen. Prostitutes, willing and able, are always ready, for a price, to cater to a man's every desire. It is simply cheaper and definitely far less risky to fulfill one's sexual desires and phantasies with a professional prostitute than with an unwilling partner.

DeKok broke the stunned silence.

"Afterwards she fled from the room," he went on. "She was crying and ran through the temple. Brother Cornelis, her uncle, intercepted her. Furious, upset and humiliated, she told him about the rape. Brother Cornelis listened to her, soothed her and begged her, for the good of the Community, not to discuss the matter with others. Then he drove her home . . . That night Jessica hanged herself." DeKok paused, looked at the revolted faces of his listeners. "When Brother Cornelis heard about it, the next day . . . he swore vengeance."

* * *

They remained silent for a long time. Food and drink were forgotten and all four of them were occupied with their own thoughts. Mrs. DeKok finally rose and said she would make some coffee. The men remained in silence. It was by far the most somber post-mortem Vledder had ever attended. Strange, he thought, three supposedly hardened policemen, were made speechless by the mention of rape. But then, he mused on, it was a particularly *vile* crime.

When Mrs. DeKok returned with the coffee, Vledder finally broke the oppressive silence.

193

"How did he do it?" he asked.

DeKok accepted a cup of coffee. The warm liquid helped to drive the chill from his heart.

"The temple in Duivendrecht used to be a factory. In addition to manufacturing paint and wallpaper, there was also a disinfection department. They used it to thoroughly clean furniture and other items, before testing their products. They used a highly toxic prussic acid for the process. Brother Cornelis had found the old pipes and nozzle heads. He invited his victims to the temple under one pretext or another and then led them to one of the old disinfection chambers. Then he rendered them unconscious with the aid of nitrous oxide."

Vledder was surprised.

"But nitrous oxide . . . that's *laughing gas!*"

"Yes, indeed. The guys from the technical service discovered the cylinders. They had been coupled to the old pipes and once the victims were locked in, Brother Cornelis only had to open the valves and the chamber was soon filled with laughing gas. As soon as they succumbed, he dragged them toward the basin, entwined their arms and interlaced their fingers and then slid them into the water where they drowned."

"Horrible."

DeKok did not agree. He shrugged his shoulders.

"No, I don't think it was horrible. Cornelis gave his brothers an easy death. It was certainly not violent. They were anesthetized and simply did not wake up."

"Then what?"

"Then, in the night, he took the victims to Amsterdam in his car and unloaded them at the house the Community owned at Emperors Canal. He drove the car around the back, through the alley, arranged them on the cart and as soon the *rigor mortis* had settled, so that he could be sure they would not be separated accidently, he waited for the coast to be clear. Then he wheeled them toward the edge of the canal and slid them into the water. That part of the operation took only seconds."

Mrs. DeKok shivered.

"A macabre story."

"In a way," agreed her husband. "He told me everything this afternoon. He was also the man who painted the white 'Invalid' rectangle in the street. That way he could always be sure to reach the water's edge with his cart." He bit his lips. "I recognized the letters, I mean, the shape of the letters. They were in the same style as the block letters in the letter that led us to the sculptor, Zanderveen."

Vledder was confused.

"But why did he write you the letter and why did he give Zanderveen the commission?"

DeKok gestured grandly.

"It was never his intention to remain unpunished. That is why he originally contemplated suicide. He only wanted enough time to complete his program of vengeance."

"Still," said Vledder, "if we include Jessica, we have seven dead people, all in the name of religion. Maybe we should do away with it altogether."

"That would be a mistake," opined DeKok. "It's not religion that's necessarily bad, it's usually the people and the institutions that purport to personify religion."

"Maybe, I wouldn't know," grumbled Vledder. DeKok decided not to pursue it.

Prins had another question.

"And the statue?" he asked.

DeKok smiled at them, at his dear wife and the two eager, young men.

"Brother Cornelis had a place picked out for that," he said solemnly. "In the temple, behind the choir. As an everlasting

195

symbol of love . . . the happy love between Brothers and Sisters who believed in the Holy Blessings."